DRAGONS REALM

A 'You Say Which Way' Adventure
by
Eileen Mueller

Dedicated to my family, who enjoy riding dragons every day.

Published by:
The Fairytale Factory Ltd.
Wellington, New Zealand.
All rights reserved.
Copyright Eileen Mueller © 2015

ISBN-13:978-1519288363
ISBN-10:1519288360

How This Book Works

- This story depends on YOU.

- YOU say which way the story goes.

- What will YOU do?

At the end of each chapter, you get to make a decision. Turn to the page that matches your choice. **P62** means turn to page 62.

Will you ride a dragon? Become a wizard? Start a food fight? Beat the bullies? It's up to YOU.

There are many paths to try. You can read them all over time. Right now, it's time to start the story. Good luck.

Oh … and watch out for the evil tharuks.

Dragons Realm

A Bad Start

"Hey, Fart-face!"

Uh oh. The Thomson twins are lounging against a fence as you leave the corner store – Bart, Becks, and Bax. They're actually the Thomson triplets, but they're not so good at counting, so they call themselves twins. Nobody has dared tell them different.

They stare at you. Bart, big as an ox. Becks, smaller but meaner. And Bax, the muscle. As if they need it.

Bart grins like an actor in a toothpaste commercial. "What have you got?" He swaggers towards you.

Becks sneers, stepping out with Bax close behind. "Come on, squirt, hand it over," she calls, her meaty hands bunching into fists.

Your backpack is heavy with goodies. Ten chocolate bars and two cans of tuna fish for five bucks – how could you resist? And now you could lose it all.

The twins form a human wall, blocking the sidewalk. There's no way around them.

Seriously? All this fuss over chocolate? Not again! They've been bullying you and your friends for way too long. There's still time to outsmart them before the bus leaves for the school picnic.

A girl walks between you and the twins. You make your move, sprinting off towards the park next to school. Your backpack is heavy, but you've gained a head start on those numbskulls.

Becks roars.

"Charge," yells Bax.

"Get the snot-head," Bart bellows. Their feet pound behind you as you make it around the corner through the park gate. Now to find a hiding place.

On your right is a thick grove of trees. They'll never find you in there, not without missing the bus to the picnic.

To your left is a sports field. Behind the bleachers, there's a hole in the fence. If you can make it through that hole, you're safe. They're much too big to follow.

Their pounding footsteps are getting closer. They'll be around the corner soon.

It is time to make a decision. Do you:

Race across the park to the hole in the fence? **P3**

Or

Hide from the Thomson twins in the trees? **P5**

You have decided to race across the park to the hole in the fence.

You race across the grass.

Bart Thomson chases you, shouting, "Onto the field. Follow me."

Energized by fear, you pick up speed. The bleachers loom in front of you. You're nearly there. Racing around the back, you skid to a halt. In the air in front of you is an oval, swirling with colors, like a bubble shimmering in the sunlight.

A faint voice comes from the glimmering air. *"Help! Help me!"*

The twins' feet pound on the grass. Their breath rasps behind you.

Without thinking, you dive through the whirling colors.

The park is gone. The Thomson twins are nowhere to be seen. You're in a forest beside a river. Deep water rushes past you, gurgling past sharp rocks and disappearing around a bend.

The shimmering air you fell through shrinks and pops like a bubble.

You're stuck here, for now. You'll miss the school picnic, but at least you're safe from Bart, Becks and Bax.

Searching for a signpost or a clue to where you are, you glimpse an enormous flying creature with a long lizard-like tail in the sky. A dragon? Before you can be sure, it disappears behind a mountain peak.

Even though the river is loud, you hear that same faint voice again, *"Help me. Hurry."*

You can't tell where it's coming from. There's a trail leading into the forest and another trail along the riverbank.

It is time to make a decision. Do you:
Follow the trail into the forest? **P8**
Or
Take the trail along the riverbank? **P19**

You have decided to hide from the Thomson twins in the trees.

You race among the trees, ducking branches and scrambling around bushes. Soon you're deep in the foliage. The twins' colored shirts flash like the stripes of prowling tigers.

"Over here, in the trees," yells Becks, "I see footprints."

"We'll find the rat in no time," shouts Bart. "Follow me."

They crash through the grove, breaking branches and startling birds.

You drop to your knees and shove your backpack under a large bush with lots of undergrowth, scrambling in behind it. Scattering dry leaves, you cover your tracks and tug the grass to conceal your hiding place. Heart pounding, you freeze. Barely breathing. Listening.

The Thomsons' rough voices bellow. They stomp through the grove and thrash around in the bushes, making a racket.

"Can't find the brat," calls Bax. His voice is so close, you twitch.

"I don't want to miss the picnic," Becks whines.

"Yeah, let's go to the bus," Bart says.

Bart's the ringleader. They'll follow him. You listen to them moving away from your hiding place. Everything goes quiet. The birds start to chirp again.

Heartbeat slowing, your breath whooshes out of you. You're about to relax and crawl out of your hidey-hole, when you hear a twig snap. You freeze.

Soft footfalls sneak among the trees. The Thomsons are still there!

It was a close call. They nearly had you fooled. But they won't wait forever. They're much too impatient to hang around here all day.

Time passes. Is that them you hear? Are they leaving? Soon you'll miss the bus. Cautiously, you crawl out.

"Got you!" Bart leaps out from behind a tree, a malicious grin on his face.

You're doomed! You squeak out a useless, "Help!"

But then something crazy happens. The air around you shimmers, and a swirling colored hole appears.

"*Help is on its way!*" booms a majestic voice.

Bart looks just as surprised as you.

A blue scaly arm reaches through the hole, and scoops you up with long fingerlike talons. Bart stands with his jaw hanging open and Bax and Becks stare wide-eyed, as they come out from the trees. Then you're yanked through the hole into a cloudless summer sky.

You're hanging beneath a brilliant-blue dragon, flying over a valley filled with farms, rivers and forests. The dragon's wings are spread in flight above you, blocking out the sun. Its underbelly is pale, with a broad leather strap around it, and its strong limbs are bluer than the deepest lake. Gripped in the beast's sharp talons, your heart pounds.

The dragon could be dangerous and want to harm you. Perhaps you should struggle and get free of its grasp? Or it may be friendly – after all, it did save you from the Thomson twins.

It's time to make a decision. Do you:
Stay still because you trust the dragon? **P27**
Or
Wriggle to get free of the dragon's grasp? **P31**

8

You have decided to follow the trail into the forest.

The trail into the forest winds between massive trees with gray trunks wider than trucks. The mysterious voice is still calling, but you can't really hear it with your ears, just in your mind. Are you going crazy?

"Help me. Please."

The voice sounds desperate. Walking swiftly, you enter the trees, the tuna fish cans clanking in your backpack. You've only gone a short way when a boy, about the same age as you, steps out from behind one of the gray trees.

To your surprise, he bows. "I saw you appear out of midair. Are you a wizard?"

"A wizard?" you say. "Of course not."

"Who are you, then? I haven't seen you around before." He glances at your feet. "You've got weird shoes. Are you sure you're not a wizard?"

He looks like an urchin, with sturdy old-fashioned boots, rough-spun clothes and tangled blond hair. A sack is slung over his shoulder, and he has rope around his waist to keep his pants up.

"Um, I've just come here for a visit," you say, unsure how to explain how you got here when you don't understand it yourself.

His face lights up. "I know who you are! You're Zeebongi the Great. The old ones foretold of your coming. You came through a world gate, just like they said."

A world gate? Is that some sort of portal between worlds? "Um, I don't know how I got here."

"They said you'd say that. I'm Wil," he says, eyes shining. He bows again. "It's great to meet you, Zeebongi the Magnificent."

"I'm not Zeebongi," you protest.

"The prophecies said you'd say that too."

"My name's not Zeebongi."

"Oh, I know you have other titles," he says. "Which should I use? Wondrous One? All-knowing One? Highly Esteemed Gracious Master? Perhaps I could just call you—"

"My name is—"

"The prophecies said you'd be modest and humble," Wil interrupts, "but this is ridiculous!" He shakes his head. "I should just call you by your real name."

"Exactly." At last he's talking sense. "My real name is—"

"I know, I know!" Wil shakes his head in frustration. "Zeebongi the Greatly-Esteemed Wise and Honorable One. But I prefer Zeebongi the Magnificent. Which do you like best?"

You sigh. You're never going to get through to this guy. "Zeebongi will do." At least Zeebongi is better than the other names. Although it sounds like some sort of kid's toy you get with a burger.

"I'm on my way to Dragons' Hold to become a dragon rider," says Wil. "Where are you going, Zeebongi?"

Dragons' Hold? A dragon rider? Maybe that *was* a dragon you saw in the sky. Scratching your head, you say, "Actually, I heard a peculiar cry for help coming from along the trail and thought I'd see who it was."

"Help." The voice sounds fainter, as if the owner is exhausted.

"There it is again," you say.

"I didn't hear anything, but I will aid you in your great quest, Zeebongi." Wil bows. "I am ever at your service."

A whimper comes from deeper in the forest.

"I heard that," says Wil.

Of course he did. That whimper wasn't in your head – and it was loud. "Come on, we have to go."

You run along the narrow trail with Wil close behind. He's fit and keeps up easily as you pelt through the woods, following the voice. Ducking around a bush, you startle a hare. Birds warble strange songs. Wherever this place is, it's not somewhere you've been before.

"Help, please." The voice in your head sounds closer. You stop and look around. "Wil, it's coming from somewhere nearby." You wave your hand to the right. "I think we need to search here."

Wil tilts his head. "Now it's stopped whimpering, I can't hear anything." He steps off the track towards where you motioned.

You follow him, scanning the ground in front of you and looking through the trees. Stumbling over a tree root, you land face-first on the ground, near a bush.

"Watch out!" the voice pipes up. *"You nearly squashed me."*

"You're amazing," says Wil, his eyes glazing over with adoration, "that was the perfect dive."

You ignore him. Turning your head, you see a glimmer of purple under the bush. Two yellow eyes stare back at you. It's some weird creature that you don't have at home.

"I knew you'd help me," its voice sounds in your head.

Scrambling to your knees, you push the foliage back. Your eyes nearly fall out of your head. On the leaf litter, under the scrub, is a purple dragon about as long as your forearm!

"A dragonet!" Wil exclaims over your shoulder.

Although you've seen dragons in books, you'd never thought they were real. Heart hammering, you slowly stretch out your hand.

"I'm Aria," the dragon says. *"Thank you for coming."* She zips out from under the bush and clambers onto your forearm, wrapping her tail around your elbow. She's trembling.

"Aria." You stroke her back and she lets out a throaty rumble, but keeps shaking.

Wil jumps back, shocked. "You heard a dragonet

talk?"

You nod.

"It called you?" he asks.

You nod again.

"You mind-melded with a dragonet, *without touching it.* And you tried to tell me you weren't Zeebongi." He sighs. "I wish I had dragonet-finding powers too. All my life I've wanted to ride a dragon. That's why I'm going to Dragons' Hold."

"I don't have dragonet-finding powers," you say.

"Then how did you find it?" Wil frowns.

"I just heard her calling me."

"Her?" Wil looks at you as if you've gone mad.

Perhaps you have. It's been a very weird day. "Her name's Aria," you tell Wil. "She told me so."

Aria whimpers. *"I'm lost. I fell out of my mother's saddlebag and landed here. I'm lonely and hungry and need to go home."*

You stroke her again. "You're hungry, are you? Poor girl."

"You're so lucky, Zeebongi," says Wil. "I've always wanted to ride a dragon, and now you have a dragonet riding on you." His eyes shine with excitement. "If she's hungry, let's feed her."

You set the trembling dragonet down, and open your backpack. "Um, Wil, what do dragons eat?"

"You're testing me, aren't you, Zeebongi?" Wil laughs. "Meat, of course. But I only have bread and cheese. Do you have any meat?"

Aria, sitting among the flowers, opens her jaws, then snaps them shut.

"See that?" says Wil. "I know almost as much about dragons as you, Zeebongi."

What's he talking about? You stare at Aria, who snaps her jaws again.

"She's practicing to make fire, even though she's too young to flame yet." Wil beams proudly, as if he's just passed a school test with a perfect score.

"I'll be old enough to make flames soon," Aria says in your head, reminding you of little kids at school.

You chuckle and tip out the contents of your backpack to search through all that chocolate for the cans of tuna fish.

Wil stares at the shiny chocolate bars. "What are they? Is that metal?" He picks one up.

"Be careful," you say, "it bites."

He yanks his hand away.

You laugh. "I was only joking!"

He looks relieved. "I didn't think I could see any teeth. But then, I wasn't sure." He stares at the contents of your pack suspiciously.

"I have some fish in this metal box." You show him the can of tuna fish. "But it's pretty hot. I'm not sure if Aria will want it."

"How can it be hot?" asks Wil. "Is there a fire inside?"

"No, just some chili."

"Chilly? You mean that it's cold?"

"No, where I come from, chili is a type of pepper." You pull the tab on the tuna fish can and show him.

He wrinkles his nose, then pokes at the chocolate wrapper again. "You're sure it doesn't have teeth?"

"I'm sure." You open the chocolate and hold it out to him. "Here, have a smell."

Wil takes a deep sniff and his face lights up. "This smells great." He licks his lips.

You break off a piece of chocolate and give it to him. "It's called chocolate."

Wil pops the chocolate into his mouth. His eyebrows nearly hop off his head in surprise. He gives you a chocolatey grin. "This is good."

Aria perks up, nostrils twitching. *"Can I have some too?"* She stares at the chocolate. *"I'm so hungry."*

"No, Aria, that isn't for you." You're not sure if you should feed a baby dragon chili. But tuna fish has got to be better for her than chocolate.

You take a spoon out of your lunch box and carefully select a chunk of tuna fish without too much chili on it. Holding the spoon out towards Aria, you coax her towards you.

"Aria, come and have something to eat. I have some fish for you."

"Strange fish," she replies, taking a few tentative steps

towards you.

She sniffs the spoon and sneezes. Will she reject it? Suddenly she gulps everything off the spoon, then leaps over to the can, and gobbles up the lot – tuna fish, chili and all.

"Wow, that was fast," you mutter.

Aria's body goes stiff. Her eyes spin. She roars. Flames shoot out of her tiny maw, blasting past Wil. She takes off, streaking along the path, leaving a scorched trail of grass behind her. Grabbing your water bottle, you douse a patch of flame. Aria shoots straight up in the air. She somersaults, her flames die, and she lands in the grass.

You and Wil rush over to the tiny creature, whose sides are heaving. Glancing at Wil, you start to laugh.

"What is it?" he asks.

"Your face is sooty."

"So is yours."

You wipe the back of your hand across your face. It comes away black. "I thought you said she couldn't breathe flame yet?"

"She shouldn't be able to until she's much bigger." Wil's eyes are large. "It must be that magic pepper-fish you gave her."

"It's not magic, Wil."

"Then what is it?"

It's no use, he's not going to believe you if you tell him about fishing boats, canning factories and chili plantations.

"That was fun," says Aria. *"Have you got any more?"* She burps loudly. Her belly is round, distended with food.

"I think you've had enough for today, Aria."

"I agree," says Wil, wiping his face with his sleeve. "But perhaps I can have another piece of that choklick?"

"Can I try some too?" Aria rolls her eyes, looking cute, but you shake your head.

"No way. If that's what chili does to you, I'm not about to give you a sugar rush!"

While you and Wil have some of his cheese in thick slabs of his homemade bread, you face the next problem.

"Wil, Aria said she's lost her mother and needs to get home, but I have no idea where her home is."

"That's easy," Wil speaks around his mouthful. "All dragons live at Dragons' Hold. That's where I'm going. I can take you both with me."

You hesitate. What about going home? "Wil, how can I find another portal?"

"A what?"

"That shimmering air that I came through."

"Oh, you mean a world gate?" He squints at Aria. "My ma says dragons have something to do with world gates, but my da says it's wizards who create them."

Aria ignores him, staring at you. *"You have to come too,"* she says, stamping her foot. *"I made a world gate to save you from those horrible bullies, now it's your turn to help me."*

She's right. She did help. Now it's your turn. "Alright, Wil. Aria and I will come with you. Where is Dragons' Hold?"

Before Wil can answer, Aria pipes up, *"Here, inside Dragon's Teeth."*

A ring of ragged mountains appear in your mind, as if you're flying over them. You swoop over the jagged peaks and down over a basin, flying over wilderness, forests, a silver lake, and farmlands. Dragons speck the sky, riders on their backs. Others sit on ledges, up the mountainside at one end of the valley. People dot the fields, and work in fruit orchards. *"This is Dragons' Hold."*

Wil is talking, "… so we'll just have to decide whether we stop for supplies on the way or not."

"Sorry, Wil. I missed most of that. Aria was showing me Dragons' Hold."

"You're so lucky, Zeebongi. I wish I had a dragon." Wil sighs. "I will, soon. I was planning to walk to Montanara, to get a few supplies, and then go on to the blue guards."

"Blue guards? Do they have blue skin?" Anything could be possible in this world.

Wil laughs. "No, they ride the blue dragons who take folk into Dragons' Hold. That's the only way in, and if you want to be a rider, you need to see them. But now you're here, we might have enough supplies to bypass Montanara and go straight to the blue guards." Wil eyes your backpack.

You open your pack again. Inside are the chocolate bars, four cookies, a mini-pack of potato chips, some dried fruit, and one more can of chili tuna fish.

Wil pokes at the potato chips and leaps back when the foil packet crinkles, shaking his head. You laugh, and he grins. "No teeth either!" he says.

He opens his bag and shows you half a loaf of bread and a small round of cheese, wrapped in cloth.

"Do you think we have enough?" he asks. "It's half a day's walk to Montanara, but if we get bad weather or run into trouble, it could take us days. Perhaps we should go for supplies. Wise Zeebongi, it is up to you."

Aria pipes up. *"I want to go straight to the blue guards. Their dragons are my mother's friends. They'll help us get to Dragons' Hold faster."*

Wil thinks you should go for supplies, but Aria wants to go straight to the blue guards. If you go straight there, you may not need supplies, but if you are delayed, you might not have enough food.

It is time to make a decision. Do you:

Go to Montanara for supplies? **P67**

Or

Go straight to the blue guards? **P89**

You have decided to take the trail along the riverbank.

The trail follows the river then heads across a meadow into the trees. As you reach the tree line, a girl steps out, holding a bow with an arrow aimed straight at your chest. Was hers the voice you heard?

"Halt!" she calls.

No, it definitely wasn't her voice. You raise your arms in the air, mentally groaning. You've fled from three bullies, just to confront an archer.

The girl is a little taller than you, dressed in brown and green old-fashioned clothing with a dark green cape. Her hair is in braids and she's wearing hand-stitched boots. She narrows her eyes and looks you up and down. "What is that strange garb you're wearing? And where are you from?"

"What do you mean, *strange garb?*" you ask. "You look pretty strange to me. Are you on your way to a costume party or something?" But her arrowhead looks sharp enough. She's a real archer, alright.

She beams. "This is my new apprentice cloak." She's obviously proud of it.

"It's the nicest apprentice cloak I've ever seen." It's the only one you've ever seen, but you don't tell her that.

She looks you up and down again and lowers her arrow slightly, but still keeps it nocked. "Because you've been so polite, I won't shoot you straight away. Come with me. My master will want to meet you."

"Your master? Who's that?"

Her eyes glint. "It's obvious you're not from Dragons' Realm or you'd know Master Giddi. Now, take that strange rucksack off."

Dragons' Realm? Nowhere near your neighborhood, then. You drop your backpack, wishing you'd taken time to eat some of your picnic when you'd first landed on the grass.

She gestures with her arrow towards the trees. "Step away, over there."

You move back to lean against an enormous tree, as wide as a car. The bark is smooth and gray, harder than any tree at home, and warm from the sun.

The girl drops her bow for a split second. A moment later she's wearing your backpack, her bow and arrow trained on you again. She's fast. You have no chance against her, unless you can distract her.

"Walk," she barks, "just in front of me. And no tricks. My arrow's trained on you."

You gulp, and go further along the trail. One false move and you'll have an arrow through your back. Perhaps you were better off with the Thomson twins.

"What's your name?" you ask.

"Mia," she snaps. "Keep walking."

Your attempts to chat with her go nowhere, so you

walk in silence, passing many more of the huge trees. You step past plants you've never seen before – bushes with vivid orange and yellow flowers shaped like parrot beaks, others with long thorns, and ferns towering above your head. Where are you? What is this weird place with odd flying creatures, unusual plants and strangely-dressed people? Perhaps it's a movie set. Or some sort of virtual reality show. Or maybe it's real. Maybe you should've followed the trail into the forest, then you might have found out who called you through the portal into this strange place – at least you wouldn't have a mad archer following you.

Thwack! You jump as an arrow flies past you, thudding into a tree. Brown muck splatters your cheek. Was Mia aiming for you, or for something really dangerous – a snake or poisonous scorpion? You can't tell from the remains pinned to the tree, but it must be pretty dangerous because she's gone pale.

"What was it?"

"March!" she barks, tugging her arrow out of the tree and cleaning it on the ground.

You keep going. An arrow whooshes past your head, nearly piercing your ear. Another arrow flies into the undergrowth. She yanks it out before you can see what she's hit.

No doubt, some dangerous creature. Swallowing hard, you stutter, "Th-thank y-you for protecting me." Your heart pounds as she continues to march you down the trail, her bow up, ready for more perilous beasts.

Wump! What an awesome shot! Her arrow hits a trunk right in front of you, piercing the body of a hairy spider. Its legs struggle then flop still. She grunts and retrieves her arrow.

Why would she shoot a spider?

Suspicious, you ask her, "Are you scared of–"

"Keep walking," she snaps.

A few minutes later, she calls, "Halt! Use that large stick and clear the path." Her arrow gestures to the trail ahead.

"There's nothing there," you say.

"Do as I say," she barks. Her bow is shaking.

Why is she so scared? Walking forwards, you see fine gossamer threads in a beautiful pattern, blocking the way. It's a spider's web.

You glance back at Mia's pale face. "Are you scared of spiders? And their webs? Have you been shooting spiders the whole time?"

"Of course not." Mia glares.

You stifle a laugh. Yeah right! No wonder you didn't see what she'd been shooting. Her enemies were so small! You bite your cheeks in an attempt to not laugh, but a snigger escapes you.

"It's not funny." Mia blushes.

Her bow stops shaking as you break down the spider

web with the stick, and clear the path. By the time you're finished, you're laughing out loud. "I thought you were killing scorpions or venomous snakes, or poison dart frogs – not spiders."

She laughs too. "No wonder you were looking so worried!"

"Look, Mia, I don't want you killing every spider in this forest, so I'll just move them out the way with my stick."

"But–" She sighs. "Oh, alright, then."

As you walk, you flick spiders out of the way, sending them flying into the undergrowth. It's a relief that Mia's arrows are no longer whizzing past your head, although you can't believe such a brave archer is so terrified of tiny spiders. Finally you come to a clearing in the woods. A small cabin is nestled on the edge, a faint wisp of green smoke rising from its chimney. Green smoke? Now you know you're nowhere on earth.

Before Mia can march you up to the cabin, the door bursts open and a man appears. He reminds you of a toilet brush, tall and thin with bristly hair that sticks up. He's dressed similarly to Mia, but his cloak is longer, nearly touching the ground, and is a weird shade that flickers from green to brown and back again.

His dark eyes flash and his laughter booms across the clearing. "Aha, Mia, so I was right! There *was* a disturbance by the river." He looks you up and down. "A world gate, by the look of things. Let's see who it's delivered."

Without warning, the man raises his hand. Sparks shoot from his fingertips. Halfway across the clearing, they burst into green flame. You duck. The flames narrowly miss your ear, leaving a warm glow as they pass.

He waves his hand again and a ball of green flame rushes towards you, aimed at your chest. You try to duck, but can't move fast enough. In panic you raise your hands. A flash of light shoots from your palms, extinguishing the fireball.

The cloaked man's deep laughter bounces across the clearing.

You stare at your palms as if they are aliens. What just happened? They've never emitted light before. After a moment you look up at the chuckling man. "Um, … Mister Giddi?"

"Master Giddi," he says, bowing.

"Head of the Wizard Council," Mia adds.

A wizard? This place is really odd. You move closer to the trees for protection. Glancing at Mia, you remember she's his apprentice. Her arrows were probably the least of your problems.

Master Giddi stares at you for a moment. "You showed good mettle just now, not running when I sparked you, and some raw talent, defending yourself with a flash-shield."

A flash-shield? Is that what just happened? Self-consciously, you glance at your hands again, wondering when the next blast of light will shoot from them.

Master Giddi's eyes rove over you, as if he's measuring you and memorizing his calculations. After what seems like forever, he says, "I'm looking for a few more apprentices. Would you like to learn magic?" He snaps his fingers and a fireball hovers in front of him. Waving his hand up and down, he bounces it in the air, then flings his arm outwards.

The fireball shoots across the clearing, heading straight for a nearby tree. Master Giddi snaps his fingers again and it extinguishes.

That's awesome. You have a chance to learn magic. To control fire! Before you can answer, your hair and the nearby leaves are stirred by a strong breeze. A whooshing noise comes from overhead. A huge bronze dragon spirals down and lands in the clearing. Its scales gleam in the sunlight. You've never seen such an awesome creature.

A soft "wow," escapes your lips as you duck behind a tree.

A young man – dressed in a hooded brown jacket, tight-fitting trousers and boots – swings down from the dragon's saddle. He strides over to Master Giddi and claps him on the shoulder. "Hello, Master Giddi." He nods at Mia. "Handel and I are heading to Horseshoe

Bend to pick up some arrowheads from the blacksmith. Do you need any supplies?"

You can't see anyone else. Handel must be his dragon.

"Great to see you, Hans," says Master Giddi. "We're fine, but we do have a visitor…"

You step out from under the trees. Hans stares at your sneakers and jeans, frowning. "Such colorful shoes and strange clothes," he says. "Did this person come through a world gate?"

"I suspect so." Master Giddi nods to Hans, then his dark eyes rest upon your face. "You could go to Horseshoe Bend with Hans and Handel if you prefer not be my apprentice."

"Fine with me," says Hans, "but we'll need to go. I have to be back at Dragons' Hold soon." He walks towards Handel, and climbs up into the saddle.

What a choice! If you stay with Master Giddi, you'll learn to summon fireballs and use your flash-shield. Maybe Mia can teach you some archery. But if you go to Horseshoe Bend, you'll ride a magnificent bronze dragon and see more of this strange land of Dragons' Realm.

It is time to make a decision. Do you:
Stay with Master Giddi and become an apprentice wizard? **P34**
Or
Go with Hans on his dragon to Horseshoe Bend? **P43**

You have decided to stay still because you trust the dragon.

Mountains ring the valley with their vicious jagged peaks. A cold breeze bites into you, tugging at your clothes, trying to sneak inside. Wrapping your arms around the dragon's forelegs, you snuggle against its warm skin to break the wind. You'd expected its scales to be cool and rough, not comforting, like soft worn leather.

The dragon roars and a rumble courses through its body, making your skin tingle with excitement. Rushing towards you are dozens of dragons of all colors, frolicking in the air. Their riders' shouts echo off the mountainsides, bouncing around you in a strange medley of whoops and hollers.

In front of you, the air shimmers – another portal. Your chest tightens. Surely you're not going back already? Your adventure has only just begun. The portal warps as a blue dragon appears, clutching someone in its talons.

"Put me down, you monster!" It's Bart Thomson, a terrified grimace on his face. "Take me back. I want to go home."

Another blue dragon pops through the portal holding Bax in its talons. "Yahoo!" yells Bax, grinning. His dragon swoops. "Yeehar," cries Bax. "This is fun!"

Becks comes through the portal grasped by yet another blue dragon. There are dragons of all colors wheeling in the sky around you. Most of them have riders, but only the blue ones are carrying people in their talons. In fact, as you look more carefully, you realize that all of the blue dragons are holding people – all about your age. The blue dragons fly to a vast ledge outside an enormous cavern halfway up a mountainside. Your dragon swoops, depositing you there.

Awaiting you is a tall woman with dark hair. Like the other dragon riders, she is dressed in brown trousers and a thick jacket. Behind her, at the mouth of the cavern, is a silver dragon.

"Welcome to Dragons' Hold. I'm Marlies," the woman says. She has extraordinary turquoise eyes. "These are our imprinting grounds. The young dragons will be here soon, and if you're lucky, you'll form a lifelong bond with a dragon and it will choose you as a rider."

"Wow," you murmur. "I could imprint with a dragon? And become a dragon rider?" You've heard of imprinting, the special bond forged between animals and humans. It would be awesome to fly a dragon through the skies.

The dragon holding Bax drops him to the ground and he rolls to his feet. "That was great," he says, coming over to you. "Where are we?"

Although you don't trust Bax, you figure he won't hurt you in front of a dragon rider. "Dragons' Hold. This is Marlies." You gesture at the woman. "And this is Bax."

"Dragons are cool," says Bax. "Flying with that dragon is the best thing I've ever done."

"Welcome, Bax." Marlies smiles, her turquoise eyes lighting up like sun on a lake. "Come and meet my dragon, Liesar."

Bax eagerly follows Marlies into the cavern at the back of the ledge to meet the silver dragon.

You wander to the front of the ledge. Blue dragons swoop past you, setting people down. The blue dragon with Becks arrives. She rushes over to join Bax in the cavern.

The dragon holding Bart swoops in to land. Bart struggles to get loose and falls out of the dragon's clutches too early. His foot hits the edge of the ledge. He stumbles, losing his balance. Bart flies over the edge, saving himself by grabbing a rocky outcrop. The blue dragon bats its wings and lunges at Bart, but rocks are in the way so it can't get hold of him.

"Help," cries Bart. "Help me up."

Memories flash into your mind – Bart teasing you, tripping you, stealing your lunch money, cheating on tests and getting your friends into trouble. Becks and Bax always joined in, but he was the ringleader. You look down the steep cliff side at the valley far below. If you do nothing, Bart will die. He'll never bother you at school again. You're all here in Dragons' Realm, miles away from home. No one will ever know.

30

But your family has taught you to be kind to others, even if they aren't kind to you.

It is time to make a decision. Do you:

Save Bart? **P198**

Or

Do nothing and let Bart die? **P187**

You have decided to wriggle to get free of the dragon's grasp.

The dragon roars and a jet of flame shoots from its maw. Not sure that you want to be in the clutches of such a ferocious beast any longer, you wriggle and try to squirm your way free, but it's clutching you too tight. It's probably just as well, you're way too high to survive a fall.

As if the dragon can read your mind, it tucks its wings alongside its body and plunges into a headlong dive towards a forest below. You gulp! Hard! Has the dragon rescued you from the Thomson twins just to dash you against the treetops?

Water streams from your eyes as the air rushes past, but you're too petrified to blink. The trees rush ever closer. You cling to the dragon. Just when you think you're about to be impaled upon the spike of a dead tree, the dragon lets out a rumbling chuckle and swoops upwards, then down over the edge of the forest towards a river.

Perhaps the river is a better place to be dropped. The water may cushion you. Nope, on closer inspection that's a roaring river, deep with a strong current. The dragon goes lower. Its grip loosens and you ready yourself for the cold wet plunge.

The dragon's talons start to open. You take one last breath.

The dragon flings you up and over the river. Oh, no! Your fall will not be cushioned by water. You're going to fall on land. Unable to help it, you squeeze your eyes shut, then open them as you land on your back in an enormous haystack.

Hay is much harder than you thought. But much better than drowning in a swift river, being dashed on treetops or plummeting onto land. The dragon circles you twice. From the haystack you see that the strap around the dragon's belly was to hold a saddle in place, and there is a rider astride the brilliant blue beast.

The rider waves, and calls, "Good Luck." It is the same deep booming voice that you heard through the portal.

The dragon roars, belching forth a blast of flame, and takes off over the forest leaving a smoking trail behind it.

Now that you have time to think, you understand the dragon probably wasn't going to harm you. It rescued you from the Thomson twins, and when it knew you didn't want to stay in its talons, it dropped you in the safest place possible.

The haystack is on the edge of a narrow field that runs alongside the river. Still wearing your backpack, you slide to the ground and brush the hay off your clothes.

There is a dense forest to the rear of the field and a track leading from the field along the river. You have no idea where you are, or how to get home, but maybe the trail leads to a cottage or a village where you can ask for help. As you're trying to decide what to do, you hear a faint voice calling, but you can't tell where from. Was it the dragon rider again? There's nobody in the sky. Perhaps it was just the water you heard?

Striding across the field, you walk to the river's edge. Water chuckles over jagged rocks lining the riverbanks. You're glad the dragon didn't drop you on those. A rotting jetty sticks out into the river, with a slimy raft tied to it. A pole lies under a sign that says: *Use at Your Own Risk*.

You could use the raft and see if you can find anyone along the river. Or you could walk along the trail by the riverbank.

It is time to make a decision. Do you:

Take the raft and go down the river? **P127**

Or

Take the trail along the riverbank? **P19**

You have decided to stay with Master Giddi and become an apprentice wizard.

By the time Hans and Handel have left, you're ravenous, so you open your backpack and pass Mia a peanut butter sandwich, which she frowns at and sniffs.

"How did you cut the bread so thin?"

"We just buy it like that," you tell her as you munch your sandwich.

Her frown turns to a smile as she tastes peanut butter for the first time.

You take out two bars of chocolate, open one, and give a piece to Master Giddi.

"Smells delectable," he says, flicking his fingers at the chocolate on his palm. It floats into the air and hovers in front of his mouth for a moment before he snaps his teeth over it. "Delicious."

Mia agrees. "If I'd known you had this stuff in your rucksack, I would've taken it back at the river, before Master Giddi got any of it." She waves her finger and a piece of chocolate hovers above her mouth. A flame ignites from her forefinger, melting the chocolate so it drizzles over her tongue.

"It's called chocolate." You slide another bar into your pocket.

"I don't mind what it's called," says Mia, "just keep

feeding it to me."

"Time for training." Master Giddi leaps to his feet.

Mia pokes a chocolatey tongue out at him. "Oh, alright."

Master Giddi laughs then addresses you. "Let's get your fingers sparking before nightfall." One of Master Giddi's bushy eyebrows rises. "Mia, the first step is... ?"

Mia sighs and gets up. This is obviously basic stuff for her. "To sense the energy around you."

"Alright." Master Giddi waves his arm at you. "Stand with your eyes closed and breathe deeply. Listen to your heart beating. Feel how it pounds, sending blood around your body. Now feel how your life energy pulses outward into the world. Feel your roots to the earth flowing out of your feet, down deep into the ground. Sense how everything connects."

The birds chirp in the trees. The sun is warm on your face, but you can't feel any roots sprouting from your feet. You stand forever, waiting for something to happen.

"Eyes shut," Master Giddi snaps.

How did he know you were about to open them?

"Focus!" he says. "Feel your pulse throbbing to nature's beat. Sense yourself in harmony with the world. Sense the trees, their energy, each of them part of one great—"

This isn't working. You open your eyes. "I can't feel anything. Just me."

"It takes time, close your eyes again."

Master Giddi repeats his instructions over and over. Each time, you feel nothing, no surges of energy. None of the stuff he's talking about.

Finally, the master wizard touches the tip of your pinkie with his forefinger. "Try this." As Giddi raises his finger, your pinkie is pulled upwards, and you feel connected. In fact, you feel a whole lot more.

Your fingertip pulses. You feel the stretch of your nail growing, and the blood coursing through your hand. The sensation grows stronger, flowing down your arm and into your chest cavity. Life force pulsates through you.

Leaping into the air, you cry, "It's true. It's true."

Mia rolls her eyes. "Don't get too excited," she says, "you haven't even made a spark yet." Casually, she flicks a few green flames across the clearing. They land in a pail of water next to the cottage, sizzling.

"That's a good start," Master Giddi nods at you. "But you need to learn to feel the energy yourself, all the time. We need to test you under pressure and see what you sense then."

Mia steps forward. "Master Giddi, I have just the trick." She winks at him and picks up her arrow and quiver. "May I?"

Master Giddi smiles. "Why not? I'll see you both at sunset for supper." He passes you a small knife in a sheath. "Mia will protect you, but you can't go into the forest unarmed." You slip the knife into your pocket.

Mia dons her bow and quiver, and motions for you to follow her into the forest.

"Where are we going?"

"A place where you can focus." Her grin makes you think that she's about to play a prank on you, but Master Giddi said you should go, so you follow her, holding a stick to ward off any spiders.

You come to a grove of the same large gray-barked trees that were near the river.

"These are strongwood trees," says Mia. "You need to hug one."

"What? I'm not a tree-hugger!" You shake your head. "No way, Mia, you can pull your prank on someone else."

Mia sighs. "Listen, it's part of your training. Giddi made me do the same. I felt ridiculous, but it works. If you want to create flames and fireballs, strongwood trees are the fastest way to access environmental magic."

You'll have to trust her, so you make your way to the nearest strongwood tree. Tentatively, you stretch your arms around it and lean your cheek against the smooth bark. The tree is warm, just like the one near the river, even though this one is in the shade. Closing your eyes, you focus on your pulse, feeling the blood running through your veins. This time it's easier to feel your connection with the earth and this tree.

Something thuds into the trunk next to your face. Your eyes fly open. An arrow is embedded in the tree, just in front of your nose. You whirl, jumping back.

"You nearly killed me!" you yell.

"No, I didn't." She looks bored. "Actually, I could've pierced your nose if I chose to, but I was aiming for the tree. You'll notice I hit it." She sighs. "I bet you lost your focus. You really should concentrate better."

You open your mouth to protest, but she's right.

It is time to make a decision. Do you:
Stay with Mia and continue training? **P39**
Or
Dash into the forest? **P149**

You have decided to stay with Mia and continue training.

"Can you still sense the tree?" Mia asks.

"No, but…"

"Look if you're going to be any use in battle, you need to stay focused."

"In battle?" You gulp.

"It's just theoretical, most tharuks don't come too close to our clearing, but you never know…" she says.

"Tharuk? What's a tharuk?"

"You don't know what a tharuk is?" Mia shakes her head. "They're monsters."

Real monsters? The sooner you learn magic, the better. "Let's get on with this."

Something skitters across dead leaves. It's loud. "What's that?" you ask. "Could it be a tharuk?"

"No, it's nothing," Mia says. "Let's get on with training. Go and stand over there."

A dog-sized spider runs out from the trees. Its body is brown with yellow stripes and it has huge fangs. No wonder Mia is terrified of them. You wave your stick at it, and yell, "Mia, quick, your bow and arrow."

"What for?' she says, as cool as cucumber.

"The spider!"

The spider skitters over to Mia, and she pats its head. "Off you go," she says. The huge arachnid scuttles off

YOU SAY WHICH WAY

into the forest. "It's only the small ones you have to worry about," she says. "They're still poisonous when they're little. By the time they get to this size, you can reason with them."

She's mad! Your knees are still shaking. You glance around nervously. "But—"

"Let's get on with it. You can face me, or you can hug the tree," she says. "Which do you prefer?"

"I'll face you." That way you might see the arrows coming.

Mia tugs a round red fruit out of her pocket. "Sit against the tree." You cross your legs and lean back against the trunk. She places the fruit on your head. "Now close your eyes and focus. Tell me when you sense the energy of the tree and of the forest."

The tree thrums against your spine. "I feel it," you call.

"Keep concentrating," she says, "and keep the pomegranate on your head."

An arrow thuds into the tree above you. And another.

Sitting straight, you balance the pomegranate, not moving your head, as the arrows whiz past you. Soon they come closer, disturbing the air near your cheek. Mia had better be careful or she'll hit you. You feel the energy around you building, the thrum of the tree growing stronger.

The next arrow stirs your hair. Hopefully she's just about finished with this stupid game.

Then an arrow hits the pomegranate, shattering it. Sticky fluid sprays over your head and face. Your eyes fly open, stinging as juice dribbles into them. Red seeds are splattered all over your T-shirt, jeans and hands. That's enough, you've had it. Mia is going to pay for this.

Furious, you stand, and point at her. "Mia, you're such a–" Sparks flit from your fingertip. You stare at them. How did they get there? The thrumming inside you builds, and a tiny flame bursts from your fingernail. Your jaw drops.

Mia laughs. "You did it! You harnessed environmental energy, that's great!" She drops her bow and runs towards you, grinning, her nimble feet dashing over dry leaves. Suddenly, the leaves swirl. A net yanks Mia into the air, suspending her from a strongwood tree. A bell on the net rings out.

"Tharuk trap," Mia calls from the net, her face pale. "The monsters will be here any minute. Quick, run for Master Giddi."

Ominous snorts come from the trees. It's too late. The monsters are nearly here.

"Hide in the trees," hisses Mia.

Scaling the strongwood tree that Mia's net is suspended from, you hide among the foliage.

A furry creature sneaks around the tree, edging towards Mia. It walks on two legs and has clothing, like a person, but has tusks like a warthog's, and beady red eyes. It swipes long claws through the air in a vicious slash, narrowly missing the net.

Mia stretches her fingers between the woven ropes, flinging flames at it.

The fur on the creature's chest catches fire. The tharuk bats at the fire, howling, and snarls at Mia. "I'll be back soon, weakling," it spits, "then we'll see who's stronger."

Mia shoots a tiny fireball after the retreating beast.

"Hurry up, do something." Mia says. "We've no time to get Master Giddi. You have to get me out of here."

What can you do? Desperately, you ferret in your pockets and pull out two items. A chocolate bar and the knife Master Giddi gave you. If the knife was bigger, you could slash Mia out of the net in a moment. But it isn't. It will take ages to free her with such a small blade.

Perhaps, if you offer the tharuks chocolate, you may be able to tame them.

"Hurry," calls Mia, "they'll be back soon."

It is time to make a decision. Do you:
Cut Mia out of the net with your knife? **P101**
Or
Offer the tharuks your chocolate? **P105**

You have decided to go with Hans on his dragon, Handel, to Horseshoe Bend.

"Climb up," says Hans, reaching down towards you from Handel's back.

A moment later you're upon Handel, in the saddle behind Hans, who waves to Giddi and Mia. The pungent smell of leather fills your nostrils. The dragon's huge bronze wings unfurl and you feel the power in its muscles as its legs bunch. Then you're airborne, heading for the trees.

You duck to avoid being hit by branches, but the mighty creature flicks its tail downwards and flaps its wings so you clear the treetops. Below you, Mia and Giddi wave. You let go with one hand to wave back, then Handel swoops, speeding up. You grab Hans around the waist so you don't fall off.

The sun glints off Handel's bronze-scaled wings. The forest is a carpet of blurred green below. Far in the distance, a range of snowy mountains glisten in the sun. You gasp in awe at the amazing view.

Hans pries your fingers off his belt and guides your hands to clasp each other around his waist. "Loosen up there, I need to breathe." He chuckles. "First dragon ride, is it?"

"Sure is." You flex your cramped fingers. "It's awesome." Far behind you is a river winding between the trees and further beyond, vast plains. Here and there, threads of smoke wind up through the trees, perhaps solitary cottages like Giddi's. "I can see so far, see everything."

"It's quite different to being on the ground, isn't it?" calls Hans, the wind whipping his words past your ears. "I don't think I could ever go back to living without Handel."

The dragon rumbles, its body resonating beneath you, and looks back, shooting a tiny spurt of flame from its maw.

"Dragons and their riders can mind meld." Hans says. "It's even better riding a dragon when you know what it's about to do. Hold on tight!"

Hans leans forward and you squeeze his waist. A village is tucked among the trees, tendrils of smoke rising up to greet you before dissipating. Handel pulls his wings into his sides, flicks his tail up and dives head-first towards a grassy clearing. Wind rushes into your face, whipping your hair back, and making your eyes water. Your heart pounds. How can Handel stop in time?

Just when you think you're about to crash into the treetops, Handel swoops and circles the clearing, slowing as he descends, then landing gently on the grass. Breath shudders out of you, half in relief, half in excitement.

Hans laughs. "Handel, you cheeky monster, that may have been a bit too much for our guest." He slides out of the saddle and helps you down, leading you around to Handel's head. "I think Handel should apologize." Hans places your hand on Handel's forehead.

A voice rumbles in your mind. *"It was a pleasure giving you your first ride. I can sense you enjoyed it. Let me know any time you'd like another."*

WOW! A dragon spoke to you using telepathy. You grin and nod. "I'd love another ride some time, Handel."

Hans laughs and scratches Handel's nose. "You rascal, that wasn't exactly an apology. I'll be back with the arrows soon." He takes you across the clearing to a trail that winds through the trees. "I guess you haven't been to Horseshoe Bend, given that you're new around here."

"Why is it called Horseshoe Bend?" you ask. "Do they have a lot of horses here?"

"Good guess. But, no, it's because the Spanglewood River has a huge bend in it, shaped like a horseshoe, south of here. This is the nearest settlement. Sturm, the local blacksmith, is one of the best — he crafts fine swords and good arrowheads." Hans gives you a shrewd glance. "He has a son about your age called Mickel. Perhaps you'd like to spend some time with him?"

"That would be great."

Between the trees, you glimpse crude cottages with thatched roofs, and hear pigs grunting. An overwhelming stink drifts on the wind, making you wrinkle your nose.

"Only the best entrance for dragon riders," says Hans,

rolling his eyes, leading you past a rudimentary fence around the pig sty. "Just breathe through your mouth until we're upwind." He winks. "And smile at the settlers even though the pigs stink."

Stink is an understatement. You've never smelled such a pong – it's even worse than Bart Thomson's feet in gym class.

Settlers stare at you. Children dressed in simple clothing, often with rope for belts, run up to greet Hans and tug your brightly-colored T-shirt – a gift from your cousin before he went missing two months ago.

It's really weird having everyone stare at you and touch your clothes. You blush, wishing something would happen to make them stop staring – anything. Even a detention would be better than this.

As you pass the sty, a pig squeezes between the fence palings and breaks free, oinking and charging towards you. Startled, you freeze. The pig leaps up, puts its muddy forelegs on your jeans, and chews on your T-shirt.

Hans pushes the pig back down. "Out of here."

Something hits your butt. You spin and can't believe your eyes. A goat, thankfully hornless, is taking another run at you. Its head is down, hooves smacking the dirt. You jump to one side but, ow! The pig has joined in, charging at you too.

You take off, racing between the crude dwellings and run into a flock of chickens, which take to the air and follow you, squawking and pooping. Shrill oinking cuts through the chickens' squawking. Oh, no! A whole horde of pigs is charging at you, the T-shirt muncher in the lead.

The settlers laugh as you spin and take off in the other direction, trailed by chickens, a mad goat and a pog of pigs.

A boy with a broad chest and huge well-muscled arms runs towards you. "Just keep running," he says, "I've got this."

The settlers cheer. He dashes past you and suddenly a pig goes flying over your head and lands in the muddy sty. Another pig follows, flying through the air, squealing like a – well, like a stuck pig – before splatting into the mud, grinning. The pigs are having the time of their lives. You skid to a halt beside Hans. The boy is slinging pigs in a rapid blur. Then he shoos the chickens away and tucks the goat under his arm, striding towards you. The settlers applaud him, then turn and go about their business, as if tossing pigs is perfectly normal.

A couple of children can't resist one last tug on your T-shirt. You can't help wondering what your missing cousin would think of everyone tugging the shirt he gave you.

"Hi, I'm Mickel," the boy says, holding out his free hand for you to shake. Under his other arm, the goat bleats. "Welcome to Horseshoe Bend."

Shaking his hand, you say, "I never thought I'd see pigs fly." You pat the goat.

Hans laughs. "Neither did I! They flew nearly as far as Handel. Mickel is the blacksmith's son I mentioned earlier. I'll call by the smithy in a few hours and see how you're both doing." Hans waves and leaves you with the strange, but very strong, pig-flinger.

"Um... thanks for helping me." You can't help glancing at Mickel's bulging biceps as he absent-mindedly lifts the goat up and down in the air like a weightlifter.

"No problem." Mickel grins. Three small children form a queue next to him. Without a break in the conversation, he lifts a kid too, working out both arms. "You new around here? You look like one of those other-worlders."

"Um, yeah, just came through a world gate," you reply, trying to sound cool. He looks so ridiculous lifting a goat and a child.

"We had another other-worlder here for a while," says Mickel, "but he went off to Dragons' Hold with Hans."

"Dragons' Hold? What's that?"

The other two kids grab hold of Mickel's thighs – one each – and he does sumo squats, giving his legs a workout while keeping up his overhead presses. This is really over the top. Totally OTT. Utterly ridiculous.

Mickel answers you as if weightlifting three children and a goat is totally normal. Perhaps it is. "Dragons'

Hold is where Hans and Handel live, with hundreds of other dragons and riders, including Zaarusha, the Dragon Queen, and Anakisha, the Queen's Rider."

"A Dragon Queen?"

"Didn't you think Handel was magnificent?" Mickel asks.

"Handel was awesome."

"Well, Zaarusha is even more beautiful. They say every one of her scales shimmers with the colors of the rainbow."

This place is incredible, so different from home. Your trip on Handel was amazing, one of the best experiences of your life, and now you've found out that there are hundreds of dragons, some even more beautiful.

"How did you get so strong?" you blurt out. "Uh, sorry, I didn't mean to be rude. It's just—"

Mickel winks. "I had problems with bullies and had to do something."

Your eyes fly open in amazement. "Bullies? *You* had problems with bullies?"

Mickel shrugs. "Yeah, everyone wanted to challenge the blacksmith's son to a fight. I used to lose, until I learned two things."

He's so open and friendly, you find yourself telling him things you'd normally never tell a stranger. "I get bullied by the Thomson twins, back at home."

Another child leaps onto Mickel's back, clinging to

him like a backpack. He hardly seems to notice, and just keeps exercising. "I can teach you both of the things that helped me," he says. "What would you like to learn first – the secret to developing strength fast, or how to fight like a warrior?"

You frown. What would be most use against the Thomson twins? "Can you tell me a little more?"

"Sure," says Mickel, putting down the goat, and shaking the children off his back and legs as if they were breadcrumbs. He's still holding one child. "Although I honestly think that most problems can be solved by talking."

"Not with the Thomson twins," you reply. "Bart Thomson has only one volume – yelling – and his vocabulary consists of a lot of grunting."

Mickel absent-mindedly keeps lifting the child to continue his overhead presses. The kid grins. "Giant John is the best fighter in Dragons' Realm. He lives in the woods near here and loves new students," Mickel says. "Or I can show you the secret to getting strong quickly." Mickel winks again.

"Well, I think I'd like to – ow!" The goat butts your bottom. Not again!

"Oops," says Mickel, "I put the wrong kid down."

He lets the child go and snatches up the goat again – then carries it to a nearby pen. "What do you want to do first?" asks Mickel.

Learning combat skills will definitely help you face Bart Thomson, but so would being stronger.

It is time to make a decision. Do you:
Learn Mickel's strength-building secret? **P52**
Or
Train with Mickel and Giant John? **P58**

You have decided to learn Mickel's strength-building secret.

Being stronger will help you face the Thomson twins when you get home. "I think I should build my strength," you say.

"Great decision," says Mickel, approaching you. "Do you mind?"

Mind what? Perhaps he's going to whisper the strength-building secret in your ear. "Sure, no problem." You lean towards him and suddenly find yourself upside down as he hoists you into the air and throws you up on his back. You're sitting on his shoulders with your legs hanging down his chest, like a little kid.

"A shoulder ride? That's your secret? How can that make me strong?"

"This isn't my secret," he laughs, gripping your calves so you don't fall off. "This is just transport." Mickel takes off into the forest, jarring the bones in your bottom as he leaps over fallen tree trunks, scrambles up a hill and bounds through a river. You duck to avoid the branches whipping into your face.

What is with this guy? Does he just think he has the right to pick up anything or anyone and do whatever he likes with them?

"Hey, Mickel," you yell, "put me down!"

He stops near one of those huge gray trees, panting,

and puts you on the ground.

"We're here." Despite his marathon effort, he's still smiling.

"Where?"

"Here." He points at the tree. "This is my secret."

"A tree?"

"A strongwood tree." Mickel is still grinning. "And this is the biggest in the whole Spanglewood forest. That's why I train here."

"Mickel, are you mad? First you use kids as human-dumbbells, then fling me onto your shoulders, race out here like a maniac, and now you're speaking gibberish."

Mickel just shrugs and says, "Give it a try."

Could the guy start making sense? "Give what a try?"

"Want to be as strong as me?"

Do you ever. You imagine lifting Bart, Becks or Bax like human-dumbbells, and can hardly stand still.

Mickel wipes his brow with his shirt. "If you exercise in the shade of the strongwood tree, you build your strength a hundred times faster than exercising anywhere else."

Is this a prank? He probably developed his strength at the blacksmith's forge. But maybe not. His eyes look earnest as he smiles to encourage you.

You step under the tree. You don't notice anything different until you try some push-ups. Energy surges through your body, like an electric eel, making your muscles tingle. You pump your body up and down effortlessly ... ten times ... twenty ... a hundred times. After two hundred push-ups, you stop. The feeling of strength stays with you. It's like you've eaten a whole field of spinach – without getting green teeth.

Standing up, you grin, shaking out your arms. "That's incredible."

Mickel nods. "Are you tired yet?"

"No. My arms are warm, but they're not tired. This is great."

"Um, there's something I didn't tell you," says Mickel.

Oh, no. There's a catch. What is it?

"You have to exercise every second day to keep your new strength," says Mickel. "It doesn't have to be under a strongwood, although if it is, your strength will keep increasing. But if you don't exercise for two days, all your extra strength disappears."

"If it's that easy, why doesn't everyone look like you?"

"Only a few people know the secret. Some started exercising, but now they can't be bothered." Mickel shrugs. "Come on, let's do more."

You train with Mickel, doing squats and lunges while holding heavy logs on your shoulders. Your muscles tingle with that same strange electric energy as before. Next you do pulls-ups on strongwood branches, then burpies, bicep curls, and overhead presses. Mickel makes you sprint on the spot. Although sweat pours off you,

you still feel great.

Mickel takes you to a nearby stream for a drink. "That should be enough training. You're looking good."

Your arms do feel firmer, your legs feel like they could run a marathon.

"Now that you're stronger, let's test your new speed," says Mickel. "Race you to the settlement."

It's never been as easy to run.

Following Mickel, you race between the trees, jumping across the river in one bound, and leaping over logs. Mickel laughs and you do too. That strange electric eel feeling still courses through you.

Long before you get to the blacksmith, the metallic clank of a hammer hitting an anvil rings through the air. The forge is joined to a stone cottage, and has an opening running the length of the building, with a thatched roof overhanging it. A fire blazes in a hearth. A barrel-chested man with enormous arms swings a hammer onto a piece of glowing metal lying on an anvil. A broad-shouldered woman with well muscled-arms is holding the hot yellow-orange metal with a pair of long tongs.

"Ma, Pa," calls Mickel, "we have a visitor."

After placing the metal back into the glowing coals, Mickel's father and mother come outside. His ma smiles. "Welcome to our hearth. I'm Hanishka, and this is Sturm."

Sturm grasps your hand, squeezing your fingers in his strong grip. You're glad you've just trained under the strongwood tree, otherwise your poor fingers may not have survived. Mickel winks, obviously thinking the same.

"I see you've been training in Mickel's favorite spot, developing your strength," says Sturm, "You're welcome to stay with us and keep developing your skills. We have a spare bed."

Mickel grins even wider than he's been grinning all day.

Hans comes around the corner of the forge. "Sturm, I've got my–" He sees you. "Oh, you're back. I have all my arrows. I just picked them up from the fletchers, now I'm ready to go."

Sturm says, "Hans and I have been talking. There was a lad that came through a world gate a while ago. He's now living at Dragons' Hold…"

Hans' piercing green eyes regard you. "You can come to Dragons' Hold with me and meet him if you like."

Dragons' Hold sounds great. Hundreds of dragons and riders, a dragon queen, and a person from your own world.

"Or you can stay here, with us," says Mickel, "and I'll show you all my smithy secrets." He winks as he says *secrets*. You know he can make you strong and help you beat Bart, Bax and Becks if you ever get home.

"Come on," says Mickel, "I'll walk you and Hans to the clearing while you think about it."

It is time to make a decision. Do you:
Stay with Mickel? **P143**
Or
Go to Dragons' Hold with Hans? **P111**

You have decided to train with Giant John.

"I need to learn how to fight. The Thomsons broke Bobby McGraff's arm a while ago."

"That's awful," says Mickel. "Giant John's training would help you stand up to them."

You nod. "I wish I could do both – get strong quickly *and* train with Giant John."

"You can." Mickel grins and his eyes gleam. "But we'll have to be fast. Jump on my shoulders."

He hoists you up over his head to sit on his shoulders, then he takes off, tearing through the forest, at breakneck pace. Well, you hope he won't break his neck – or yours! Ducking the branches that whip back into your face, you hang on tight. Mickel clambers over boulders, leaps streams, races across a mossy log bridging a chasm, and stops under one of the huge gray trees you saw earlier.

He pants. "If you exercise in the shade of a strongwood tree, you will increase your strength one hundred times faster than exercising anywhere else."

"You're joking!"

"No, I'm not. Watch this."

Mickel swings you into the air, using you like a dumbbell to do overhead presses. The trees around you bounce like yo-yos, but it's you that's moving, not them.

"Alright! I believe you," you gasp.

"Great!" Mickel puts you down. "Let's start training."

You both drop to all fours to do push-ups. As soon as you start exercising, a jolt goes through you, like touching an electric fence, and your muscles buzz with energy. Instead of doing ten or twenty push-ups, you manage hundreds without feeling tired.

"This is amazing."

"To keep your new strength, you have to exercise every second day," says Mickel. "It doesn't have to be under a strongwood. If you don't exercise for two days, all your extra strength disappears."

"Sounds fair enough. Exercising daily will be easy with this extra strength."

Mickel grins. "I know. Come on, I'll teach you a quick trick before you meet Giant John. Then you can surprise him when he suggests you spar with him."

"Sounds good. What is it?"

"Push me," says Mickel.

You reach out to shove him. He grabs your arm and a moment later, you're on the ground. "Oof!" Air rushes out of you and you gasp for breath. "How did… you… do that?"

Mickel pulls you to stand. "Grab your opponent's arm with both hands, using the momentum of their push to pull them towards you, like this." He gestures for you to push him again, then yanks your arm, pulling you off-balance. "Next, trip them, and their body weight will do the rest – as long as you're quick enough to jump out of the way." He demonstrates.

Once again, you're eating dirt. Leaping up, you say, "Let me try."

You yank Mickel forward and trip him, but he lands on top of you. "Ow! You're heavier than you look!"

"You need to move faster," he says, dusting himself off. "As you trip them, duck out the way."

You try again. Mickel lands flat in the dirt!

"Wow! This is awesome!"

"Come on, you need to practice a few more times, then we have to get going."

A while later, you're sprinting through the forest at Mickel's side, soon arriving at a thatched cottage in the woods.

Thuds and yells ring through the air – the sound of people fighting. Mickel rolls his eyes. "There must be a better way to solve all this conflict. I get so sick of using my fists to solve problems. Perhaps we should see whether Giant John wants to teach us mediation?"

"Come on, Mickel," you say, yanking him towards the clearing.

"Alright," he says, "but remember to trick Giant John with those new moves."

You burst through the trees into a clearing. Four people are fighting, in pairs, with wooden staves.

"Giant John," Mickel calls out. "I have a new recruit."

An enormous guy is bashing staves with a familiar

figure. It's Giant John fighting Bart Thomson. The other two are Bax and Becks, and they're going like crazy, whacking each other.

You groan. Now you'll have to fight them all, and they'll have a great reason to give you a solid thumping. What rotten luck!

Giant John drops his staff to come over, but Bart is quicker. Tossing his staff aside, he races towards you. "Hey, Fart-face, wondered where you got to."

Frozen, you stare at him. He looms above you, larger than life. Behind him, Bax and Becks rush over. Bart lunges, arm out to shove you.

Your reflexes snap into action, strongwood strength zinging through your muscles. Grabbing Bart's arm, you yank him forward, trip him and twist out of the way. You're stronger than you think. Bart flips over your head and sails through the air. He lands on his back in the middle of an ant nest. Insects swarm over him.

What were you thinking? Now Bax and Becks are going to pulverize you. Your muscles are tight with tension.

Bax swings a punch. You grab his arm and a moment later he lands, dazed, against a tree trunk. A squirrel hops onto his chest, and bites his nose, as if it were a nut. "Hey!" yells Bax, then catches it, stroking its back.

Becks hangs back, frowning. "Something's changed," she says, scrutinizing you.

Bart rolls around to squash the ants, then clambers to his feet. His usual glower has been replaced with raised eyebrows. "You've been learning a few tricks." His eyes appraise Mickel, taking in his strong arms, and then flit back to you. He whistles, obviously impressed.

"Nice to meet you," says Bart, extending his hand to Mickel.

Your jaw drops. Bart is never polite. Ever.

Bart nods at you. "Well done, Fart-face. You bested me." He wanders back to the clearing to grab his staff.

You can hardly believe it.

Bax shakes your hand too, and strolls over to Bart, his new pet squirrel chittering on his shoulder.

Becks narrows her eyes, turns, and stalks off after her brothers.

Mickel raises an eyebrow. "Are these the Thomson twins?"

You nod.

"But there are three of them. They aren't twins, they're triplets."

"Shh," you whisper, "they can't count that well."

He laughs.

Giant John shakes your hand. "You've learned well." He shoots a shrewd glance at Mickel, who just grins. Giant John looks at you. "I gather you know my three newest pupils? It looks like they've been bullying you in your world. Is that right?"

"Um, yeah. This is the first time I've beaten them."

"Nothing like training under a strongwood tree, is there?" Above his dark beard, Giant John's eyes twinkle. "Let's forget learning staff, knife and bow techniques – that way they can't hurt anyone seriously." He scratches his beard. "That move you just did was one of my old wrestling tricks. How would you like to learn more?"

More cool moves to outwit Bart, Bax and Becks? That sounds great. Although, from the anxious looks Bart is shooting you, you may not need to learn many more tricks. Bart seems positively nervous. You try not to grin. You never thought you'd end up stronger than him.

Smiling at Giant John, you say, "Good idea. Can we start now?"

During the next hour, Giant John and Mickel take the four of you through basic wrestling techniques. Giant John stresses how important it is to obey the rules and be fair to those who are weaker. Much to your amazement, for the first time in their lives, Bart, Bax and Becks are model students – although Bart's feet still smell.

When Giant John is done, Mickel says, "Hans is expecting us back at the forge. Who wants a race?"

The Thomson twins yell in glee and take off after you and Mickel, dashing through the forest. Mickel takes a much more direct route home, a mad race through the trees and over a rickety bridge back to Horseshoe Bend. Much to the amazement of the Thomson twins, you run through the settlement with Mickel, flinging happy pigs into their sty, and weightlifting children and goats. The settlers laugh, greeting you both.

Bart, Becks and Bax are sweaty and panting as you reach the forge. You and Mickel are not even winded, as if you'd just taken a stroll.

The metallic clank of a hammer hitting an anvil rings through the air. The forge is joined to a stone cottage. A fire blazes in a hearth. A barrel-chested man with enormous arms swings a hammer onto glowing metal lying on an anvil. A broad-shouldered woman with well muscled-arms is holding the hot yellow-orange metal with a pair of long tongs. Hans is packing arrows into a sack.

Mickel points at the forge. "Those are my parents."

Hans steps outside the forge. He looks you over and raises his eyebrows, smiling. "Been training, have you? And found some more other-worlders. It's time to decide what you're doing next. All of you, come with me."

Hans leads you through the settlement, past grunting pigs and squawking chickens, to the clearing, where Handel is preening his bronze scales.

Bart Thomson looks startled. "Um…" He stares at Handel. "Is that thing safe?"

Hans chuckles.

"Bart's been terrified of animals since he was a kid," says Bax, earning himself a dirty look from Bart.

That's handy information. You file it away for when you get home.

"Handel wouldn't hurt a dragonfly," says Hans. "Unless it harmed one of his friends."

You walk over to Handel and put your hand on his nose. "Nice to see you, my *friend*," you say.

Your meaning isn't lost on Bart. "Um, nice d-dragon," he says.

Handel laughs in your mind. *"He's been a little annoying, has he? Let me know if he gives you more trouble, and I'll sort him out."*

Hans clears his throat. "I know you've enjoyed yourself here, but I think it would be best if you live with more other-worlders. There was a lad that came through a world gate a while ago. He's now living at Dragons' Hold. You can come with me to Dragons' Hold and meet him if you like."

Dragons' Hold sounds great.

Hans' piercing green eyes regard you. "Or you could go home. Handel can create a world gate for you to return, right now."

Bart blurts out. "Can we go home, please, now?"

He's just said *please*. Amazing. Handel must really impress him. You scratch Handel's nose. "If I go home, I'd love you to visit me on Earth, Handel," you say out loud, making sure Bart gets the message. "The more often, the better."

A rumble of pleasure courses through Handel and he spurts a tiny playful flame at you.

You swear Bart's knees are shaking. If you do go home, things are bound to be different from now on.

A whirling oval of shimmering colors appears in the air near Handel. Bart shoves Becks and Bax – squirrel and all – through the portal, then glances back nervously before he leaps through too.

It is time to make a decision. Do you:
Go home with the Thomson twins? **P175**
Or
Go to Dragons' Hold with Hans? **P111**

You have decided to go to Montanara for supplies.

"We can't risk running out of food on the way," you say, walking along the trail. Aria wolfed down the tuna fish in such a hurry, you're sure she'll need more food soon.

"I want to see the blue guards and find my mother." Perched on your shoulder, Aria hides her head under her wing.

"I know," you reply, "but you don't want to go hungry."

A moment later she pulls her head out from under her wing and opens her jaws. Wil jumps back nervously as if she's about to scorch him, but no fire issues from her mouth, only sharp notes that trill through the trees in a crescendo.

Wil gapes at her. "Wow, I thought that I was going to get a pepper fish blast! But Aria's singing is beautiful."

Beautiful? The odd notes jangling in your ears are anything but that. You clamber over a fallen tree trunk. "Which way next?"

"Along there." Wil takes you along a narrow trail through the forest.

"What are those huge trees?" You point at the gray-barked trees that are dotted throughout the forest.

"Strongwood trees." Wil laughs. "The blacksmith's son in our village told me that if you exercise under their branches for longer than an hour, you get strong really quickly." He snorts. "But we all laughed at him."

"Was he strong?" You skirt a puddle on the track, Aria still screeching in your ears.

"Zeebongi, you don't have to keep testing me. Everyone knows that blacksmith's children are always strong." Wil pushes a low branch aside so you can pass.

You smile, even though this Zeebongi stuff is still annoying. "Did you ever try exercising under a strongwood tree?"

Wil just laughs.

Aria's singing is getting flatter with every step you take. Her notes are painful.

"Oh, great Zeebongi, isn't Aria's singing divine?" says Wil. "You were so clever to find her, and now you're training her to sing so beautifully."

Trying not to roll your eyes, you move Aria from your shoulder to your forearm to save your ears. "Aria, you look tired. Would you like to sleep?"

"Of course not!" she yawns. *"I'm calling my mother. Every dragon recognizes their dragonet's song. She should be here soon."*

She starts singing again, off-key and flatter than before. Even though you enjoy having a dragon, you've had enough of this terrible squawking. The sooner Aria's mother comes, the better.

Wil smiles. "I should've known she'd be a great singer. After all, her name is Aria."

Maybe Wil is tone deaf. Or can't hear at all. "Wil, you have such good taste in music!" you say. "Not," you mutter under your breath.

"Thanks," says Wil, missing your sarcasm.

"Wil," you ask, "have you heard a lot of music before?"

"Not much," he answers.

"That explains it."

"What?" says Wil.

"Ah, nothing." If you only had your MP3 player, you could teach him something about *real* music.

The longer you march, the worse Aria's singing gets. Finally, you have a brainwave. "Let's eat," you say. That way her mouth will be full and you won't have to hear her sing.

After the bread and cheese from Wil's sack are finished, you get out a chocolate bar. Wil's eyes light up, and so do Aria's. She snaps the chocolate out of your hand and gulps the whole bar in one swallow, wrapper and all, then gives a happy roar.

Wil beams. "Wow, Zeebongi, you're so clever! She liked that." Then his face falls. "But she didn't leave any for me. I wanted another piece."

"So did I!" But without the wrapper.

Aria's eyes spin faster and faster. She roars again, then scampers up your arm, and leaps onto Wil's head.

"Hey!" yells Wil.

Aria jumps into the air, flying off into the forest. She zips in and out of the trees, zigzagging around like a crazed chicken. You both watch her, grinning.

"She's gone crazy," mutters Wil, "absolutely crazy. I've never seen a dragonet acting like that."

"But I bet you've never seen a dragonet on chocolate before. Maybe they'll all be like that if we feed them chocolate."

Wil sighs. "I don't suppose you have any more choklick?" He licks his lips.

You wink. "I do, but don't tell Aria."

The dragonet roars and zooms out of the trees, crashing on your outstretched legs.

"That was fun," says Aria, *"but now I'm tired."* She burps and leaps onto your arm, only to start singing louder than before.

It's your fault. The chocolate rush is making her so loud. You grit your teeth, get to your feet and start walking. "Come on," you call to Wil, "let's get to Montanara."

Aria's raucous rasping scares away the bird life. Wil whistles along with her, also off key. Now you're certain he's tone deaf. After half an hour, Aria's voice fades and she falls asleep. Tiny snores rumble through her body, vibrating against your forearm.

"At last!" You sigh in relief, gazing down at her purple scales.

"Great, isn't it?" says Wil.

Nodding, you look up and realize he wasn't talking

about Aria falling asleep. He thought you'd seen the large town ahead, visible through the last of the trees. You tuck Aria into your backpack, cushioning her with your jacket.

"Montanara," Wil says. "Our first stop is the market."

Fertile farmland stretches between the edge of the forest and Montanara. You wander along the road, past fields of wheat waving in the breeze, and reach the outskirts of the town. The thatched cottages are densely-packed, lining winding streets full of people, horses and wagons.

"They're heading to market," says Wil. "It's the biggest one for miles around."

Nudging Wil, you ask, "Why are they staring?"

"They must recognize you, Zeebongi."

Sighing, you follow him past a huge wooden fence that reeks of manure. Snorts and whinnies come from behind the barricade.

"City stables," says Wil, "but I guess you knew that already, being the All-knowing One."

It's been a long day, and Wil's comments are getting tiresome, but you need him to help you reunite Aria with her mother, so you give him a tight smile, and don't say anything.

The market square is jam-packed with stalls. Over a fire, a tough-looking gigantic man is melting cheese and scraping it onto thick slabs of bread. Wil waves at him cheerily, calling, "Hi, Giant John."

Children munch roasted apples on sticks. Goats bleat as farmers milk them. Traders call out, selling their wares. Vegetables are piled high on tables and in the back of wagons, with horses tethered nearby. Brightly colored hats, shirts and cloth are for sale. You pass people haggling for the best price. With all the noise, you're surprised Aria hasn't woken yet.

You come to a stall piled high with pies and odd-shaped pastries with a spicy fragrance. Your mouth waters.

"Hey, Wil, before Aria wakes up, perhaps we should try one of those delicious-looking pastries."

"Sure, Zeebongi," says Wil. He pulls some copper coins out of his pocket.

"Zeebongi?" mutters a peasant woman next to you.

"Zeebongi!" says a farmer behind.

"Yes," exclaims Wil, "this is the Greatly-Esteemed Wise and Honorable One."

"Zeebongi!" someone calls. "Zeebongi!" Murmurs fill the busy market square.

Around you, people fall to their knees, their arms stretched up in worship. The haggling comes to a stop. Traders cease yelling mid-sentence. Children drop their apples as they fall to their knees. Even the animals go quiet.

"Hail,' says Wil, jumping up onto the edge of a wagon.

"Zeebongi the Magnificent will speak to you."

You roll your eyes. He's been wanting to use the *magnificent* title all day. After all, he admitted it was his favorite. "There's no need for all this fuss," you call. "Carry on as usual."

Just then, Aria awakes and sticks her head out of your backpack. You open it and she climbs out, onto your shoulder, unfurling her wings.

"A dragonet!" someone calls.

The crowd murmurs.

Wil nudges you. "The prophecy said you'd be good with dragons."

Above the crowd's prostrate bodies, on the far side of the square between a stand of hats and a table piled high with vegetables, a large furry gray creature appears, dressed like a warrior. Black saliva drips from its tusks when it sees Aria.

"Tharuk!" The cry ripples through the crowd.

Someone hisses, "Fast, hide the baby dragon."

Another furry creature appears behind the first, then a whole troop enter the market place. Beside you, Wil is pale. It's the first time you've seen him without a grin. Those creatures must be bad.

"Dragonet!" bellows the first tharuk, pointing at Aria. "I'm hungry! Seize it, now!"

Still upon the wagon, Wil leaps into action, waving his hands at the crowd. "Stand up. Create chaos. Protect the

Great Zeebongi and his dragonet."

The crowd surge to their feet. Nearby, someone lets a cage of chickens loose and they flutter into the air around you, flapping their wings, clucking and squawking. Traders bellow at the top of their voices. Children dash between the stalls, shrieking.

Wil ducks a barrage of chicken poop. "Quick, Zeebongi! Do you want to hide here in the market or over in the stables?"

The market has many potential hiding places – any stall could provide cover – but the tharuks are already here, searching for you. You could give them the slip and go to the stables, but will other tharuks be waiting on the road outside the market square, ready to catch you?

It is time to make a decision. Do you:
Hide in the marketplace? **P168**
Or
Run to the stables to hide? **P75**

You have decided to run to the stables to hide.

You snatch Aria off your shoulder and tuck her under your arm. "Quick! To the stables," you yell, dashing between the stalls, dodging children and horses. A few stray chickens are still flapping and cackling in the air, hopefully giving you cover. Around you, the bellows of monsters compete with shrieks and screams. Without time to glance back, you can only imagine the chaos.

Will leaps over a goat sitting in his path and leads the way to the road. You follow, racing down the cobbled streets. He wrenches the stable yard gates open and you sprint inside, only to come face to face with the Thomson twins.

Bart is shoveling a pile of horse manure. Becks is carrying a wooden pail of water and Bax is currying a horse, whistling. All three of them are wearing clothing similar to Wil's – simple brown trousers and shirts.

Bart looks up. "Fart-face?"

Wil puffs himself up, looking angry on your behalf. "That's no way to talk to the Great—"

Aria burps loudly, cutting Wil off before he can say *Zeebongi*. She winks at you. *"I thought that would stop him."*

Thankfully she was so quick. You don't want your whole school to call you Zeebongi when you get home – if you ever get home again.

"What are you doing here?" you ask.

"It's all Bart's fault." Becks scowls. "If he hadn't jumped through the portal and stolen some pies, we wouldn't have been forced to work here as punishment."

Bart sneezes. "And I'm allergic to horses."

The horse Bax is grooming snuffles in his pockets. "We're so glad to see you. You're the first normal person we've seen all day." Bax pats the horse's nose. "Wow, is that a dragon?"

"Yeah, her name's Aria. We need to hide. Tharuks want to eat her."

Behind you, Wil bolts the doors to the stable yard. "Are these your minions?" he asks.

Bart scowls.

"Wil, these are the Thomson twins. Bart, Bax and Becks, this is Wil."

"Great Zeebongi," whispers Wil, "I hate to disagree with you, but they're triplets, not twins."

"Ssh, don't tell them that!" you whisper back. "They can't count!"

Thumping sounds on the gates. "Open up," roars a throaty voice.

Wil's face is panic-stricken.

"Quick," says Bax, "follow me." He runs to the stalls.

Aria flies after him. You follow with Wil. Bart and Becks go about their duties as if there weren't any monsters banging on the gates. The bashing on the gate gets louder.

Snorts and soft whinnies sound in the dim building. Horses shove their noses over stall doors to greet Bax.

"Always liked animals," says Bax, blushing. "Hurry, hide in the hay." He dashes back into the yard, and is soon whistling again.

Wil runs into a stall, and dives into a pile of dung-specked hay behind a brown horse. Wrinkling your nose at the manure, you race down the corridor to an empty stall, to find a fresh haystack. Burrowing your way inside, you make a peep hole so you can see. In the stall opposite you, Aria leaps into some hay to hide.

The gates creak as Bart opens them and greets someone. A moment later, the door to the stables is flung open.

"No, sir, there isn't anyone in here," says Bart. "Just a few horses, sir. See?"

"Think I'm fool enough to search filthy manure, do you?" Heavy stomps come along the corridor. "We all know humans are too pathetic to hide there. I'll check the clean stalls."

That's why Wil hid in that dirty hay! The stomping gets louder. The monster is coming closer.

Aria's voice pops into your head. *"I'm hiding, but I'm scared!"*

Aria's bottom is sticking out of the hay, her purple tail high in the air. Like a little child, she's only hidden her head and thinks no one can see her. It's too late to warn her. A tharuk steps into her stall.

The creature is quietly drawing its sword. You sneak out of your hiding place to save her, even though you're no match for a tharuk.

"*Oh, no!*" Aria says in your head. Her bottom twitches.

Rumbling shakes Aria's stall. A jet of brown gas and shredded streamers of blue-and-silver chocolate wrapper fly out of Aria's bottom. A pooey chocolatey stench overpowers the scent of horse. The tharuk stumbles back, clutching its nose as a shower of chocolate-wrapper-confetti rains down on its head.

You never knew dragon farts had such power!

Startled into action, you yell, "Aria, here!"

She zips into the air, hay trailing around her, and flies over the tharuk's head to your stall. Yanking your backpack open, you pull out the chili tuna fish and she gulps it down.

Roaring, the tharuk leaps up, snatching at Aria. Flames spurt from Aria's maw, straight at the tharuk's chest. Its clothing catches fire. The stink of burned fur fills the air. Again, the brave dragonet darts at the beast, flaming the monster's ears.

"Ow!" The tharuk clutches its ears and runs down the aisle.

Clank! Bart steps out of a stall and hits it on the head with his shovel. The beast crumples to the ground. Only then do you smell burning. A spark has caught the hay.

It's frightening how fast the small flame is growing.

"Becks," you yell. "Water!"

Becks runs in with her pail and douses the fire. Wil clambers out of the filthy hay and joins you all, stomping on the steaming ashes.

The tharuk groans. He's coming around.

"We need to leave. He's got buddies." You cautiously open the stable door. There's no sign of the other tharuks. Yet.

An enormous wagon loaded with produce rumbles into the yard, horses snorting. Upon the seat is the giant you saw melting cheese in the marketplace. He leaps from the wagon and flips down the side, revealing a hidden compartment under the floor.

"Giant John!" cries Wil, still covered in strands of manure-coated hay. "Can you get us out of town?"

"Hop in," says Giant John, clapping Wil on the shoulder. "It'll be a squeeze, but I can hide you."

On the street outside you hear the roars of more tharuks.

It is time to make a decision. Do you:

Escape in Giant John's wagon? **P80**

Or

Stay in the stables and confront the tharuks? **P88**

You have decided to escape in Giant John's wagon.

From his worn leather boots to the knife in his belt, Giant John looks exactly like the sort of person you shouldn't accept a lift from – especially in a hidden compartment in his wagon. As if picking up your thoughts, Wil nudges you towards the wagon.

"It's alright – I've known him all my life. You can trust him."

The tharuks are getting closer, their boots pounding the nearby street. It's a no-brainer really. Besides, Giant John looks tough – tough enough to handle a few tharuks, and the hidden compartment in his wagon is brilliant – much safer than fighting those beasts.

"Quick, jump in!" You gesture at the wagon and look at Wil.

Before Wil has a chance, Bart, Becks and Bax squeeze into the compartment, jamming themselves up against the far side. You let Wil go next, so you're not right next to the Thomsons, then you clamber in.

"Aria, come on."

She's trembling on the ground, eyes whirling. *"I hate tight spaces."*

"Come on, you'll be alright."

Giant John scoops her up, pops her in next to you, and snaps the side of the wagon shut. He thumps his way up onto the seat and the wagon rolls across the stable yards and out onto the cobbled street. Every cobble rattles through the metal-bound cartwheels, jarring your bones.

Bart groans softly. "No suspension," he whispers.

Roars surround the wagon. The guttural voice of a tharuk yells, "Halt. What have you there?"

"You want to buy something?" Giant John answers.

All five of you, and Aria, don't breathe, awaiting the monster's answer.

"Finest onions in Dragons' Realm, these are. How many do you want? Or how about some apples?" Giant John prompts.

Thuds sound above you.

"Here you go," calls Giant John.

Something thumps to the ground beside the wagon. Tharuks snarl. There's a rip, accompanied by slurping, crunching and more snarls. The pungent scent of onions drifts through the wagon. Then the wheels start to roll again.

Aria's voice sounds in your mind. *"Giant John's so clever, distracting them with food."*

You nod, but don't dare answer in case the monsters hear you.

As you leave the town outskirts and get onto a softer dirt trail, the jarring stops, but with five of you and a dragonet jammed in together, it's getting warmer, and the smell of horse manure makes your nostrils twitch.

Turning to whisper to Wil, a piece of hay stuck to his clothing tickles your face. The pong of horse dung is unmistakable.

"Poo!" you say. "I thought that was the horse, not you!"

Wil's teeth flash white in the dark. "Sorry, it was a good hiding place, even if it was mucky."

Perhaps you should've jumped in the wagon first, then you'd have the Thomsons between you and Wil's dung-smeared clothes.

Bart farts, loudly. A cloud of stink creeps through the wagon.

Becks giggles. "Bart, that's worse than Wil's horse poo!"

After a while, the stench mingles with the smell of sweaty socks and unbrushed teeth. You hold your nose, sweat trickling down your neck in the stuffy heat.

Aria squirms. *This is torture for a sensitive dragon nose.*

"And for normal noses," you mutter as Bart lets several more farts rip.

As the journey goes on, it gets cooler. Just when you think you can't stand being cramped up in a stinking box any longer, the wagon halts.

"Could be tharuks," whispers Wil.

You all freeze. Giant John thuds down to the ground. Your heart thumps in your chest. Aria is rigid with tension. The side of the wagon flies down. Sunlight floods the compartment, making you squint. You can't see anything.

Giant John laughs. "We're here! Look at you all, a sorry lot."

Aria explodes from the wagon so fast her wingtip hits your nose, making your eyes water. You stumble out, rubbing your legs. Wil falls onto the ground behind you. Bax shoves Becks and Bart on top of Wil in his eagerness to get into fresh air.

Bart clambers up and claps you on the shoulder. "I'm so glad you got us out of there. So glad. Thanks, buddy."

Buddy? This is Bart Thomson who has never said a kind word to anyone. You nod. "No problem."

"We're here," calls Aria, flitting around in the air. *"We're here!"*

"Where?"

You don't need an answer. Several blue dragons land near a long stone building, nestled at the foot of a steep mountain. Men and women in dark clothing are on huge leather saddles astride dragons. "The blue guards," you murmur.

The dragons' scales glint in the late afternoon sun, like dragonflies. Their powerful leg muscles ripple and bunch as they walk. Although all the dragons are blue, some have lighter-blue patches, different shaped tails, or more angular heads. No two dragons seem to have the same eye color, but all their scales gleam.

"Awesome!" says Wil, striding forward to touch a dragon.

Bax joins him. Becks and Bart hang back, not looking too keen.

A woman jumps down from a dragon and strides towards you, shaking Giant John's hand. "Welcome, John. You have passengers for us?"

He nods. "I can't smuggle them back into Montanara. My wagon may be searched. And this young dragonet needs to go to Dragons' Hold."

She nods and motions to you. "Climb aboard. Aria's mother has missed her."

Soon you're behind her on the back of a dragon, with Aria on your shoulder. Wil's eyes shine behind another dragon rider. Bax and Becks are doubled up, and Bart is grimacing, hanging onto another rider as they lift off into the sky.

A dragon! You're on a dragon! This beats the school picnic, any day!

Giant John becomes a tiny figure waving goodbye as you fly up the mountainside, leaving the forest and fields behind. Montanara is only a smudge in the distance. On your shoulder, Aria starts to sing.

Once more, she's hardly melodious. Your ears ring with flat notes. "Why are you singing?"

Aria stops to answer. *"To let my mother know I'm coming! Did you know these mountains are called Dragon's Teeth? Look how sharp they are."*

If you keep Aria speaking to you, she can't sing! "What's that?" you say, pointing to the tallest mountain.

"Fire Crag."

You soar over Fire Crag and find it's part of a ring of mountains. Aria's right. They do look like dragon fangs. Nestled in a valley inside the mountains are forests and a tangled wilderness at one end, and fields and orchards at the other.

A lake glints silver, deep in the forest. And the sky is full of dragons. Dragons of all colors. The dragon you're riding roars.

Aria sings at the top of her voice, her shriek jolting through you like feedback from a microphone. From the other side of a valley, a purple shape is getting bigger. Its bellows ring across the valley above the din of the other dragons.

Soon you make out a huge purple dragon, spitting fire, and charging towards you. Aria leaps off your shoulder, airborne.

You snatch at her, nearly falling out of the saddle, and just manage to snag her tail.

"Why are you stopping me?" Aria cries in your mind. *"That's my mother!"*

"That ferocious beast is your mother?"

"Yes!"

Aria wriggles from your grasp and, singing at the top

of her voice, dives downwards. The purple dragon swoops through the air and opens its mouth. It's going to eat Aria! You scream in panic, but the dragon scoops Aria gently in her jaws, tosses her high and flings her into the arms of a rider on her back.

As you sigh in relief that Aria wasn't hurt, your rider shouts over her shoulder, "Great job, you reunited them!"

Her blue dragon roars and follows Aria's mother. Nearby, Wil whoops from another blue dragon. Bart sits behind his rider with his jaw clenched, knuckles white on the saddle. Bax and Becks are grinning from ear to ear as you all race behind the purple dragon towards a stony clearing.

Landing on the stones, the rider climbs down off Aria's mother. Aria flits to your arm. Her mother nuzzles you. Placing your hand on her snout, you hear her deep voice, rumbling through your mind.

"Thank you for bringing my daughter home to me. She's told me how you protected her. In return, I grant you permission to be her rider, when she is grown."

"Me? A dragon rider?"

The dragon nods.

"Awesome!"

But what about your family? If you stay here you may not see them, but if you leave, you won't get to ride Aria when she's bigger.

It is time to make a decision. Do you:
Stay at Dragons' Hold and ride Aria? **P195**
Or
Farewell Aria and return home? **P140**

88

You have decided to stay in the stables and confront the tharuks.

"No thanks," you say to Giant John. "I'll be fine."

"You've got to be joking," say Bart, Bax and Becks.

"Oh great Zeebongi, I'll stay by your side." Wil looks longingly at the wagon. "But wouldn't you rather leave with my good friend Giant John?"

You shake your head.

"Are you sure?" says Giant John, raising an eyebrow at you. "The tharuks will probably kill you."

You gulp. Your family told you never to accept rides from people you don't know. But Wil knows Giant John. And your parents probably weren't considering a time when you were in another world, chased by crazy monsters that could kill you.

The roaring on the street is getting closer. You have one more chance to change your mind.

It is time to make a decision. Do you:
Escape in Giant John's wagon? **P80**
Or
Face the tharuks? **P130**

You have decided to go straight to the blue guards.

"I think we have enough food, and Aria wants to get to the blue guards as soon as we can."

"I bow to your wisdom, Zeebongi," says Wil. "We need to take this trail." He pushes aside a giant fern and gestures towards a dense dark path.

You shiver as you enter the closely-packed trees. Not much sunlight filters through the treetops.

"It's creepy in here," says Aria. *"I know just the thing to cheer us up."* She opens her mouth and starts to sing. Her voice is shrill and scratchy and sounds off-key.

"Wow, that's beautiful," Wil says.

You stare at him as if he's nuts, but he doesn't seem to notice. How could he think Aria's screeching is beautiful? Stepping over a fallen tree trunk, you continue along the trail, Aria's discordant tunes jarring your ears.

Squelching through a marshy section of the trail, you take Aria off your shoulder to save your ears from splitting. Just as well, because her next tune is even more tuneless than the last. Mosquitoes nibble on the exposed parts of your skin. You slap them away, hoping this world doesn't have malaria or other mosquito-borne diseases. Dragonflies with blue, pink and green striped bodies flit in and out of the marsh grass.

Aria takes a break from singing to snap at a dragonfly.

"Aria," you scold, "can't you eat something nasty like

these mosquitoes, instead of those beautiful dragonflies?"

Aria zips off your arm and snaps at the mosquitoes buzzing around you and Wil.

"What a shame she stopped singing," says Wil. "Her songs are so melodious and I do think she's getting better. It must be your fabulous training, great Zeebongi. You're whispering hints to her when I'm not listening, aren't you?"

The guy must be completely deaf. Aria has been getting worse, not better. You can't believe that he thinks she sounds good.

"You're joking, aren't you?" you ask.

"No, I wasn't, but I can tell you a joke if you'd like me to, Zeebongi." Wil's eager smile nearly has you rolling your eyes.

"No, it's fine. I don't feel like laughing." Avoiding a muddy spot, you grab a branch and swing out to land on firm ground.

Aria lands on your shoulder and burps. "Great mosquitoes," she says. "You're right. Those dragonflies are much too pretty to eat."

"And they're called *dragon*flies," you say. "It's almost like eating your cousins. You can't do that."

Aria hangs her head. "Sorry, I won't do it again."

"I tell you what, you must be hungry, let's stop soon and have something to eat. I have some more tasty food in my backpack."

Wil's eyes light up. "Any more choclick?"

You smile.

Luckily, Aria is distracted from singing. She chatters in your mind. *"See those big gray trees? They're strongwoods. People who exercise under them grow strong really fast."*

You run your hand over the smooth gray bark. It's warm and seems to thrum under your fingers. You raise an eyebrow and keep walking.

"In some parts of the forest, there are monsters called tharuks," says Aria brightly. *"They came through a world gate into Dragons' Realm. Sometimes they kill people and eat dragonets, but I'll be safe because I'm with you."*

You swallow, wishing you had as much confidence in your abilities as she and Wil do.

"See those bees?" says Aria. *"They make the best honey in the whole realm, my mother says. Oh I'd better keep singing so she hears me and comes to find me."* Aria opens her mouth to start singing.

"Wil, here's a good place to eat," you yell, suddenly sitting down near a puddle in the middle of the trail.

Wil frowns and gives you a concerned look. Then his face brightens. "Great Zeebongi–"

"Zeebongi will do," you snap, tired of his compliments and Aria's singing.

"Zeebongi, then," says Wil. "You should have told me you were so hungry that you couldn't wait!"

"Absolutely ravenous," you say. Your trick worked.

Aria is staring at the backpack in your hands – not singing.

You pull out a packet of potato chips. Wil leaps as the wrapper crinkles.

"Remember, Wil, it won't bite."

He manages a small smile at your lame joke, but still stares at the foil as if it has a life of its own.

Aria nibbles a corner of the packet, before you can even get it open. You can't help smiling. With these two as companions, a snack will never be simple again. You pass them each a potato chip.

Aria snaps hers down in a single gulp.

Wil licks his and pulls a face. "It tastes so…"

"Salty?"

"What is salty?"

You scratch your head. "Um, salt comes from the sea."

Wil's face brightens. "I've heard of the sea. It's a long way from here."

How do you explain salt? "Well, it's um, … uh… do you like it?"

He licks his chip again. "Yes. It's very strong, but tasty."

"Wil, you're the clever one! You just explained salt perfectly."

He beams. "Me? Clever? Thank you, Zeebongi."

Aria leaps onto your arms, sticks her snout into the

packet, and slurps every last chip out. When she jumps down, the packet is still stuck on her nose. *"Help me!"* she says, batting it with her forelegs.

You laugh.

She swipes at the packet with her talons, shredding it.

Wil laughs too. "What a shame. It was so colorful. I wanted it as a Zeebongi keepsake."

Perhaps it was good it got shredded. Next he'd be selling Zeebongi souvenirs. "Come on, we should get going."

A low growl comes from the forest.

You leap to your feet. "What was that?"

"A wolf." Wil's face is tense.

"Save me!" Aria leaps on top of your head.

"Zeebongi, what should we do?"

"How would I know? You're from Dragons' Realm, not me!"

The growls get louder. It sounds like more than one wolf.

"Stop being so humble, Zeebongi. Tell us what to do!"

"Quick, climb this tree!"

A pale wolf flashes through the undergrowth.

Aria flies into the tree. You and Wil scramble up after her, grabbing low branches to hoist yourselves up. A pack of wolves break through the underbrush. They surround the tree, snarling. One leaps up, just missing Wil's leg. He yanks it to safety. You both climb higher.

Your heart is pounding. Wil's hands are shaking. Aria sits very still, her eyes whirling.

"What do we do, now?" Wil asks. His voice trembles.

You have two ideas – both are crazy, but just might work. You could feed Aria chili tuna fish and see if she can flame the wolves to scare them off. Or you could ask Aria to sing to frighten the wolves away. You can't let her know that you think her singing is awful, so you'd have to ask nicely.

A wolf howls. Others leap up at the tree, snarling.

"Quick, Zeebongi!" yells Wil. "What should we do?"

It is time to make a decision. Do you:

Feed Aria chili tuna so she can flame the wolves? **P135**

Or

Make Aria sing to scare the wolves away? **P95**

You have decided to make Aria sing to scare the wolves away.

The tree thuds as a wolf slams into the trunk, trying to shake you out. The other wolves copy it, slamming against the tree. Your branch shakes with each thud.

"Aria, I think if you sing, your lullaby may send the wolves to sleep. Would you like to try it?"

"Really?" says Aria. *"Is my singing that good?"*

"Great idea, Zeebongi," says Wil. "Her singing is so fantastic, it's sure to weave a magic spell over those rabid wolves."

Aria spreads her wings and puffs up her chest, as if she's an opera diva. Then she opens her mouth and screeches.

"Bravo," calls Wil.

"Louder!" you say. "Higher! More!"

She takes another breath and shrieks louder than you've ever heard her.

The thudding against the trunk stops. The wolves lie on the ground with their paws over their ears, whining.

Aria stops. *"Oh, they don't seem to like my song."*

"They love your singing," you say. "See how they're joining in?"

"It sounds like they're whining." Aria pouts, her lower lip sticking out like a sulky child's.

Well, she is a child, a dragon child. Now that she's

stopped singing, the wolves jump up against the tree again, thudding against the trunk, nearly shaking you off the branch. You cling on. More wolves leap up, snapping under your legs. Wil keeps his on the branch. His knuckles are white where he grips the tree.

"Aria, they weren't whining. They were singing too," You tell her. "They're just not as good at it as you are."

Aria's mouth pulls back, showing her teeth in a strange grimace. It's a dragon smile, the first you've ever seen.

"Come on, Aria," says Wil. "You're my favorite singer."

By now you're sure he's deaf! But his cheerful words convince Aria to sing again. She bellows loudly, her eyes squeezed shut, her voice squealing higher and higher, until you think your eardrums will split. The wolves are all flat on the ground, their paws over their ears. One by one, they slink off into the forest, whimpering.

Long after they've gone, you let Aria keep singing, just in case they want to return. Finally, Aria stops, exhausted. She opens her eyes and gazes around.

"Where's my audience?" she says, peering out of the tree at the empty ground around the trunk. *"I thought they'd be asleep."*

"I think wolves are creatures of habit," you say. "They must have gone home to their dens to sleep. Your lullaby worked!"

Aria snorts, and looks at you doubtfully. Then she

sniffs the air and looks skyward.

A roar echoes from above, shaking the branches. A mighty wind rustles the leaves. A purple dragon appears above the treetops.

"Mother! It's my mother!" Aria squeals in your mind. She sings again.

The purple dragon roars, and wheels away over the treetops.

"We need to follow her," Aria says.

Wil is staring into the sky at the disappearing dragon's tail. "Magnificent!" He's awestruck, clinging to the branch, unmoving.

"Come on, Wil, we have to follow her. It's Aria's mother!" you say.

"Great Zeebongi, you surely do have a way with dragons," he says. "She came to you."

"Actually, she came to Aria, because she sang," you tell him as you climb out of the tree.

"Oh, but that was your brilliant idea. Zeebongi, you truly are the All-knowing One, just like they said." He clambers down after you.

"Mother is in a clearing, a few minutes away," Aria says, flitting in front of you.

You scan the forest for stray wolves. The sooner you're near Aria's mother, the better, just in case the wolves decide earache isn't so bad after all. "Let's race," you suggest.

Wil is also glancing nervously into the forest. "Best idea you've had yet, Zeebongi."

You both run after Aria, whipping through the trees. The majestic purple dragon is waiting for you in a clearing. She has a leather saddle on her back, but no rider.

Aria flies straight to her mother, nearly hitting her nose in her enthusiasm to nuzzle her. She frolics in the air, turning somersaults and flapping around her mother's head in an excited frenzy. She's as small as a dragonfly compared to the fully-grown dragon. Her mother sits patiently, a quiet rumble coursing through her body, like an enormous cat purring, only ten times louder.

Sunlight glimmers off the dragon's scales. Its huge talons rake the grass in the clearing, like a cat kneading a cushion. Her eyes are bright green. When she turns her gaze on you, they draw you in, making it hard to look away. She seems to see through you in a glance, knowing your heart – your worst fears and your loftiest dreams.

You're filled with wonder. A dragon. A real live dragon. No one at school will ever believe this. Just as you think of school, two figures burst into the clearing.

"Watch it," shrieks Becks. "It's a dragon!"

"Wow," says Bax. "Awesome!"

"Hi," you ask. "Where's Bart?"

"Don't know," says Becks. "Last time we saw him, he was running away from a pack of whimpering wolves."

She points at Aria's mother. "Aren't you scared of that monster?"

"Aria and her mother aren't monsters." You gesture at the dragon and her dragonet – now leapfrogging over her mother's spinal ridges. "They're my friends."

Bax's eyes shine. "Can you introduce me to them?"

"Depends how friendly you are." You draw yourself up to your full height and try to look as impressive as possible.

"You should both bow before my friend here," says Wil in a haughty tone. "It's not every day you meet someone so important."

You hope he won't call you Zeebongi in front of them.

"Important?" Becks screws up her nose.

"Of course," says Bax, bowing and elbowing Becks. He's obviously desperate to befriend a dragon.

"Yes," says Wil. "Very important – my friend here mind-speaks with dragons, foretells events and even scares away wolves. Those wolves you saw were scared away by us."

Becks look impressed. She bows too.

"Do you know these people?" asks Aria. *"Aren't they the ones that were mean to you in your world?"*

You nod, knowing no one else has heard her question.

Aria balances on her mother's tail. *"Then let's send them home."*

A portal opens right near Becks.

"Time to go home," says Becks, leaping through and yanking Bax after her.

"But," calls Bax as he tumbles through, "what are we going to tell Mom about Bart?"

Aria speaks to you. *"We're going to Dragons' Hold and taking Wil. Do you want to come too? Or do you want to go home?"*

It is time to make a decision. Do you:

Go with Wil and Aria to Dragons' Hold? **P151**

Or

Follow Bax and Becks home? **P132**

You have decided to cut Mia out of the net with your knife.

The trap is suspended from the tree by two thick ropes. Lying on the branch, you reach down and grasp a rope with one hand to steady it. "Stop struggling, Mia, you're making the net swing."

"What do you expect me to do? Sit here and wait for you to free me?"

Flicking your knife open, you saw at the rope. "This should help."

"That puny little knife? Help? Fat chance!"

"You're right, but it's all I've got." It's slow work, cutting through the tough strands.

The branch lurches. You fumble, nearly dropping your knife. "Hey, are you mad? Quit moving around. You nearly knocked me out of the tree."

"Sorry, just trying to help. I should be able to reach now." Mia's arm pokes up through the net and sparks flit along the other rope.

You keep cutting, hand cramping from gripping the knife so tightly. The blade slowly frays the edge of the rope, but you're only about a quarter of the way through. Mia's rope is smoldering, wisps of smoke curling up from the brown fibers.

Grunting comes from the bushes. "They're coming!" whispers Mia. "Stay quiet. And keep cutting." A small flame bursts from her finger, setting the rope alight, but it dies out, only smoldering.

Three tharuks enter the clearing. The largest one sniffs. "Is that smoke?"

"Probably from her burning me before," says the beast with the singed chest.

Wisps of smoke from the rope curl around your face. Your nose starts to tickle. Oh, no! You're going to sneeze! The tharuks prod Mia through the net. She remains remarkably quiet. You struggle to contain the itching, but your nostrils can't stop twitching.

In an effort to keep your sneeze at bay, you remember your lessons on environmental magic and tune into the thrumming of the strongwood trees. Their energy buzzes through you, but it's no use.

"Aachoo!"

Your sneeze is so violent, you drop the knife right onto a tharuk's head. All three beasts stare up into the tree. You're cornered, trapped on a branch, with Mia stuck in a net and three monsters eying you.

It is time to make a decision. Do you:
Leap onto the tharuks' heads? **P103**
Or
Stay in the tree? **P146**

You have decided to leap onto the tharuks' heads.

When dealing with the Thomson twins, you often found the element of surprise useful. With the echo of your gigantic sneeze still ringing among the trees, you bellow and leap down towards the largest monster, hands outstretched, ready to do some damage.

To your surprise, a flash of light bursts from your hands, striking a tharuk, knocking it over, and singeing the net.

"Ow," Mia yells. "You got me too."

You crash into the big tharuk. Another stands shocked, staring at you as the burned one writhes on the ground.

Mia flings flames around the clearing and at the ropes above the net. You scramble off the tharuk, but it grabs your shirt, shredding the back with its claws. Tugging away as the animal lumbers to its feet, you take a running leap and grab Mia's net, hanging on and swinging with it between the trees. The burned and half-cut ropes creak. You let go, flying past the tharuks, landing near a huge strongwood, and roll to your feet.

You duck as Mia's net swings back, her hands still flinging fire at the monsters. They snarl and swipe at her with their long claws, ducking her flames. The half-torn ropes groan under Mia's weight and give way. She crashes to the ground, knocking over a tharuk, and scrambles out of the ropes.

Spying her bow nearby, you snatch it up and dash to her, thrusting it into her hands. But before she can fire an arrow, the tharuks have recovered from their shock and have surrounded you both, snarling. Their small red eyes flick over you. Dark saliva dribbles off the end of their tusks.

Mia's eyes are wide with panic. You strain to feel the environmental magic around you, but your heart is pounding so loudly and your knees are shaking so badly, that you can't focus.

The tharuks leap towards you as a glowing oval of colored light shimmers nearby.

It is time to make a decision. Do you:
Take Mia through the portal? **P163**
Or
Stay and fight the tharuks? **P166**

You have decided to offer the tharuks your chocolate.

Swallowing hard, you climb out of the tree to the sound of guttural grunts through the forest.

"Quick," hisses Mia. "Hide."

Ignoring her, you position yourself between Mia's net and the point where the burned tharuk disappeared into the trees.

"What are you doing?" Mia whispers. "Why aren't you hiding?"

Unwrapping the chocolate, you hold it out in front of you with a trembling hand. Your knees join in, shaking too.

"Now's not the time for a snack," Mia hisses. "Hurry up and hide."

The burned tharuk enters the clearing first, its nose twitching. Hopefully it likes the rich chocolatey scent emanating from your hand better than *your* scent. And hopefully, it's hungry – but not too hungry, you only want it to eat the chocolate!

The beast approaches, nostrils flared. "What's that?" it growls, staring at your chocolate bar.

Three more tharuks emerge from behind it, snarling and sniffing. Drops of dark saliva slide off their tusks.

"It's the best food you've ever tasted," you say, pretty sure it's true. "I'll give you a piece if you set my friend free."

The biggest tharuk snorts. "We'll take it off you anyway." It swipes its claws at you.

He's just like a scarier version of Bart Thomson — wanting to steal goodies from kids. You duck, dancing out of reach.

The beast lunges for you again, but a smaller tharuk yells, "Hey, stop that. It smells tastier than the putrid scraps Commander Zens feeds us. We should try some."

"I want some too, don't let the kid drop it," calls another tharuk.

"I'm troop leader," yells the burned tharuk. "I should get first bite. Stand down and let me deal with that human."

The large tharuk steps to one side and the burned tharuk approaches. The stench of singed fur clogs your nose, drowning out the aroma of chocolate. With nervous fingers, you break a piece of chocolate and hold it out to the monster. He spears it with a claw and pops it between his tusks into his mouth.

Roaring, his red eyes fly open and turn bright green. An enormous tusky smile breaks out over his furry face. "Delicious!" he yells. "Come on, troop, have some."

Breaking pieces off as fast as you can, you feed the other three tharuks a piece of chocolate each. They eagerly line up for more, green-eyed and beaming with delight.

Above you, Mia mutters, "What a waste of great food."

You don't have an endless supply. Thinking fast, you say, "First let the girl down, then I'll give you more chocolate."

"Let her down," the troop leader calls, mesmerized by the silver wrapper in your hand.

The other tharuks ease the net out of the tree, lower Mia to the ground, and open the net. Brushing herself off, Mia stalks over to the trees and snatches up her bow, then comes to stand beside you. "What will you do when you run out?" whispers Mia.

"Not sure," you whisper back. "Got any ideas?"

"You, troop leader," says Mia, "if we promise to feed you this delicious stuff, what will you do in return?"

Green eyes gleaming, the troop leader answers, "Anything."

"What's in that stuff?" hisses Mia. "Does it contain an obedience potion? These monsters are normally savage, but you've tamed them."

Could Mia be right? You decide to test her theory. "Um… jump up and down…"

The next minute they're all jumping on the spot.

"Great," says Mia. "Could you sing like dragons?"

They start to yowl, and one even flaps imaginary wings. Very weird. For them, chocolate is like some sort of wonder-drug. They'll do anything you say.

Mia keeps testing your theory, getting the monsters to dance and scratch their armpits.

This is great. You now have four monsters that will do anything you ask – for chocolate. You're just wondering how long the effect will last, when five more tharuks stumble out of the woods, snarling.

"What are you doing?" bellows the largest of the new arrivals. "And why are your eyes green?"

Snatching out your knife, you cut the chocolate into five smaller pieces, hoping little bits will still make tharuks obey. "Try this." You pass them each a piece.

Roaring, they stare at each other in amazement as their eyes turn green too.

Mia laughs with glee and soon has all nine of the tharuks doing as she wishes.

Suddenly the troop leader's eyes flash red and he growls a low threatening snarl. "You cast a spell on my troops! I'll get you." He lunges towards you, claws out and tusks aiming right at your face.

The air next to you shimmers, and you grab Mia's hand, ready to leap through the portal, but you can't! Something is falling out of the portal at your feet. Three somethings. The Thomson twins!

Bart falls straight onto the troop leader's back, pinning him to the ground. Becks and Bax land nearby.

"Stay there, Bart," you yell. "Keep it pinned."

The tharuk growls and snarls, but cannot move. For

the first time in your life, you're grateful Bart is so big.

Becks whirls to face you. "W-w-what are these things?"

The eyes of two more tharuks turn red, and they snarl viciously.

"Tharuks," you reply.

Becks just stares at them, but Bart yells at the monsters, "We just came from that shiny swirling air." He points at the portal. "We have an army of a hundred men waiting on the other side. They'll come when I call, so back off." He grabs one of the troop leader's ears and twists it. "And if you come any closer, I'll rip his ear off."

"You heard him," barks the troop leader. "Stand down!"

Typical Bart, bluffing so convincingly – he's fooled you hundreds of times before. "Um, Bart," you say, "they love chocolate. Got any?"

Bart snaps, "Bax, deploy the stash."

Bax unzips the bag on Bart's back and chocolate bars spill out over the ground. The only place you've ever seen more chocolate is the aisle of a supermarket.

Snatching them up, you thrust one in the hands of every tharuk, and stow the rest in your backpack. The tharuks shovel the chocolate in their mouths greedily, tossing the wrappers on the ground. Hopefully, this bigger dose will last long enough to get them back to Master Giddi. Then they'll be his problem, not yours.

"Hey, you lot," yells Becks, "do you think this is some sort of barnyard? Pick up your litter!" She points at the wrappers. "You need to be tidy tharuks and care for the environment."

The monsters smile sheepishly and pass her their wrappers. "Sorry," mutters the troop leader.

Bart and Bax are standing next to the portal, as if they're thinking about leaving. Becks is scratching the tharuk troop leader behind the ears. "Just like a big kitty-cat," aren't you, she croons. "But lots meaner – I like that."

You have the tharuks under control, but it's only going to last as long as the chocolate supply. There may also be more tharuks in the forest, so you need to find a way to keep them supplied with chocolate too. The Thomson twins could do it. Perhaps you could convince them to bring you back chocolate regularly, to keep the tharuks under control. You stare at Becks. She seems to like tharuks. Maybe you could convince her to stay, so that Bart and Bax come to visit. Or perhaps you could use your magic to convince them.

The portal starts to shrink.

It is time to make a decision. Do you:
Convince Becks to stay with the tharuks? **P156**
Or
Use magic so Bart and Bax bring you chocolate? **P159**

You have decided to go to Dragons' Hold with Hans.

"I'm going to Dragons' Hold," you tell Mickel. "Thanks for training me. I hope I get to repay you some day."

Mickel waves you farewell and leaves the clearing.

Gray clouds are gathering above the forest. "You'd better wear something warm," warns Hans, "and hang on tight."

You pull your rain jacket on over your T-shirt and climb up on Handel's back.

Handel rumbles, his body vibrating with a deep thrum, and takes off. The wind tugs at your jacket, trying to creep inside. Its icy bite easily nips through your jeans. Perhaps this ride isn't going to be as much fun as your last one with Handel.

Hans speaks, but the wind whips his words away before you can make out what he's said. Handel climbs into the sky. Your butt starts to slip in the saddle. You grab onto Hans. Then Hans throws his body forwards, holding onto purpose-built leather loops. Clinging to his waist, your head on Hans' back, you stop slipping.

The dragon climbs higher. Gray tendrils of cloud waft in front of your face, surrounding you. You can hardly see Handel, but the rough cloth of Hans' jerkin is still against your cheek.

It's spooky riding on a dragon you can't see, pressed

up against a rider you can only feel, with murky gray all around. Dampness seeps through your jeans. Your hands are freezing cold. Even your socks feel wet through your sneakers. How much farther is Handel going?

Hands and butt numb, you cling on, not daring to let go, even to rub your cold nose. Rain lashes at you, driven sideways by bitter wind. Handel swerves, trying to counter the foul weather. Perhaps you should've stayed at Horseshoe Bend with Mickel. Then you'd be in the forge next to a warm fire.

The ride seems to take forever. Gradually the rain eases and the cloud thins. You gasp. Ahead is a sheer wall of snow, rock and ice.

Hans sits up straight. "Welcome to Dragon's Teeth, the guardians of Dragons' Hold."

Below, tiny fields reach the foot of the mountains which rise into steep spiky tips, high above.

"They do look like teeth, Hans." You try to keep the shiver out of your voice, but you're so cold you don't quite manage. "How much longer until we get there?"

Hans reaches forward and opens an enormous saddlebag.

There are two in front of him and two more behind you on Handel's haunches, four in all, but this is the only empty one.

"You could climb into this saddlebag to keep the wind off..." Hans pauses for a moment.

It is time to make a decision. Do you:
Stay in Handel's saddle behind Hans? **P120**
Or
Climb into Handel's saddlebag? **P114**

You have decided to climb into Handel's saddlebag.

Getting into Handel's saddlebag sounds much warmer than sitting behind Hans, wet and freezing. Glancing at the houses dotted in the fields far below, you push down the fear clutching at your insides. If it was really risky, Hans wouldn't have suggested you move.

You scramble, bringing your knees up to kneel, then stand on the slippery wet leather saddle. Handel veers to the right. Your feet slip, throwing you off the dragon into the air.

"Help!" Flailing at a loose strap, you grab it with one hand, nearly jolting your shoulder socket from your body. "Hans, help!"

Hans looks down, obviously shocked. "Handel, quick! Rider overboard!"

Your hand slips down the wet strap, losing hold. Desperately, you grab for the leather with your other hand, but the wind whips the end out of reach. As you lose hold, the last thing you see are Handel's green eyes, whirling rapidly, beautiful against his bronze scales.

Plummeting through the cold air, the field below rapidly grows larger. Tiny beehives turn into cottage roofs. Small blobs of yellow become haystacks. Pale blue ribbons become rivers, with stones and dangerous-looking tree stumps along their banks.

Whump! With a roar, Handel clutches you in his talons and heads skywards. Relief washes over you as the river slowly becomes a ribbon once more and cottage roofs turn back into beehives.

Struggling to find your voice, you swallow. "Thank you, Handel."

Above you, the dragon shoots a lick of flames in reply.

"You alright?" calls Hans.

"Yeah." Cold and shivering, but alive – as far as you're concerned, that's alright.

Suddenly Handel drops you. You roll your eyes. Not again! Today you've done enough skydiving to last a lifetime. With a whoosh of wings, Handel dives under you and slaps you with his tail, bouncing you up into the saddle. You smack into Hans' back, your face mooshed into his shoulder.

"Oof."

"Um, sorry, Hans."

"No, I'm sorry. I was only joking about getting into the saddlebag," he says, "I thought you'd laugh, not take me seriously!"

Now he tells you! "Well, there aren't many dragons where I come from," you say through chattering teeth, "so all this is new."

"You handled that tail bounce pretty well for someone who is new to dragon riding. I'll think you'll make a fine rider." Hans reaches into the saddlebag, pulls out a green cloak, and passes it to you. "Put this on, over your damp gear."

Dubiously, you take the cloak. Your fingers instantly feel warm. Snuggling your face into the heavy material, your cheeks grow warm too. In front of you, Hans is also donning a similar cloak. You fling yours on.

"The cloak is wizard-wear," says Hans, "and contains a drying spell."

Copying Hans, you pull up the cloak's hood and feel your hair start to dry. Steam rises from Hans' hood. Soon you're warmer.

"We're nearly at Dragons' Hold," says Hans. "The home of hundreds of dragons and their riders."

"Hundreds of dragons?" you ask. "I can hardly wait."

Hans chuckles. "A few years ago, I was just like you and had never ridden a dragon, but Handel has changed my life. You'll love Dragons' Hold." He scratches Handel's neck and the dragon thrums.

Handel flies up over a jagged mountain peak. "These mountains are called Dragon's Teeth."

You're astounded. Dragon's Teeth are a ring of mountains, like an open dragon's maw. Hidden in the middle is a basin filled with farms, rivers, forests and a lake – sparkling silver in the sunlight. Dragons speck the sky, riders on their backs.

"Wow."

"Welcome to Dragons' Hold, home of Zaarusha, the

Dragon Queen, and Anakisha, Queen's Rider."

Descending, you see people in fields and orchards. Dragons are perched on mountainside ledges. A silver dragon flies towards you with a dark-haired young woman astride its back.

"Hans, who is your passenger?" she calls.

Her dragon flies alongside Handel. Both the dragon and woman have turquoise eyes. The dragon's silver scales shimmer in the evening sunlight.

"A visitor from a world gate," Hans calls. "Welcome!"

Hans looks over his shoulder. "That's Marlies. See how well she flies?" His voice is tinged with admiration.

"You like her, don't you?" you ask.

The tips of Hans' ears go red. "Of course not," he says.

"Yeah, right!" You're pretty sure Hans is sweet on Marlies.

Hans clears his throat. "See how Liesar's scales glow in the sunlight?"

Her silver scales glint like diamonds in a jeweler's window. "Liesar's awesome." You grin, knowing he's deliberately changing the subject.

Liesar spurts a tiny flame towards Handel. Wings beating, both dragons race towards the end of the valley. Liesar's tail streams behind her. The air rushes past you, making your eyes water.

Handel skims the treetops. Your heart pounds. He swoops up into the air, making your belly drop, then shoots downward towards a lake. Handel flies over the lake, dragging his talons in the water. Fine spray shoots up on either side of the bronze dragon, covering the bottom of your jeans in droplets. Luckily you're still wearing the wizard cloak.

Hans laughs. "He's washing his toes!"

Far ahead of you, Liesar roars.

"Come on, Handel," says Hans. "They're winning!"

You thought Handel was going fast before, but now trees flash past you as he zooms across the fields. Workers wave below. Liesar swoops over a field. Children cry out below, chasing after her.

"Handel," calls Hans. "Let's show those kids some acrobatics." He glances back at you. "When I say, just jump, like you did before."

"Alright." Your stomach clenches into a tight knot.

Handel shoots up into the air.

"Get ready," calls Hans.

You crouch on the saddle, hanging onto his shoulders for balance.

"Jump! Now!"

Flinging yourself into mid-air, you wonder if you've gone crazy. A stony clearing rushes up towards you. Children shriek. If Handel doesn't catch–

"Oof!" he has you in his talons again, and speeds up

into the sky, only to drop you.

To think you could've been having a picnic quietly with your school class.

Slap! Handel's tail sends you flying back into the saddle.

"Sorry," you mutter as you slam into Hans' back.

Hans laughs. "You're great! How would you like to become a dragon rider? You could join our acrobatic team. We're looking for riders who aren't afraid to try a few stunts."

You think of your family at home. Your friends. And the Thomson twins. "How would I see my family?"

"Any dragon can create a world gate back to your world when you need one."

Handel lands in a stony area at the end of the valley. People rush out to meet you, most dressed in similar clothing to Hans. Dragon Riders – men and women of all ages, and a few young ones, about your age. You could join them, become a dragon acrobat, and fly through the skies of Dragons' Realm on the back of your very own dragon, visiting your family when you want.

Or you could ask Handel to send you home now.

It is time to make a decision. Do you:

Become a dragon acrobat? **P173**

Or

Ask Handel to take you home? **P178**

You have decided to stay in Handel's saddle behind Hans.

It would be an awkward clamber around Hans, over a damp saddle, on a slippery dragon to reach the saddlebag. Looking at the very hard ground far below, you say, "Um, thanks, Hans, but I, um…"

Hans laughs. "I was only teasing!" He reaches into the saddlebag, pulls out a green cloak, and passes it to you. "Put this on, over your damp gear."

Dubiously, you take the cloak. Your fingers instantly feel warm. Snuggling your face into the heavy material, your cheeks grow warm too. In front of you, Hans is also donning a similar cloak. You fling your cloak on.

"The cloak is wizard-wear," says Hans, "imbued with a drying spell."

Copying Hans, you pull up the cloak's hood and feel your hair start to dry. In front of you, steam rises from Hans' hood. Gradually you get warmer.

Handel is gliding alongside the mountain range, steadily getting higher. Now he's not flying vertically, it's much easier to hold on.

As Handel soars over a jagged mountain peak, you are amazed that Dragon's Teeth are a ring of mountains, like an open dragon's maw. In the middle is a basin filled with farms, rivers, forests and a lake – sparkling silver in the sunlight. Dragons speck the sky, riders on their backs.

"Wow."

"Welcome to Dragons' Hold, home of Zaarusha, the Dragon Queen, and Anakisha, Queen's Rider."

Handel descends over people working in fields and orchards. Dragons are perched on mountainside ledges at one end of the valley. Handel lands in a stony area below them.

People rush out to meet you, most dressed in similar clothing to Hans. Among them is a familiar figure wearing a faded baseball cap. You climb out of the saddle and run to meet him.

"Peter?" You can't believe it. Surely it can't be your cousin. Here? Of all places?

Peter grins and grabs you in a bear hug. He looks about four years older than when you last saw him. "Hey, you're still wearing that T-shirt I gave you!"

Hans waves the crowd away, leaving you and Peter to get reacquainted. "Peter," he says, "bring our visitor inside for dinner when you're ready."

Peter nods.

"How did you grow so fast?" you ask him. "You've only been gone two months."

Peter gapes at you. "Two months? I've been in Dragons' Realm nearly five years!"

"No, you haven't."

Peter looks you up and down. "You haven't grown much, although you do look a bit fitter." He points at your muscles. "Maybe time is different here. When did you get here?"

"This morning." You glance at your watch. "About eight hours ago. I was on my way to school for our annual picnic, but ended up here. Even if I do find a way back, I've missed the picnic by now."

Peter puts his arm around your shoulders. "Don't worry, we'll have some fun here instead." He frowns. "How are my mom and dad? Have they been worried about me?"

"Yeah, police searched your neighborhood, but never found a clue. There's still a reward out."

"I hate my family being so worried." Peter bites his lip. "Is Sarah okay?" He swipes at his eyes with the back of his hand.

Sarah is your other cousin, Peter's little sister. "Yeah. She still thinks you're alive and keeps telling your parents that she sees you in her dreams, flying."

Peter laughs. "She's right. Come and meet my best friend. She's a beauty."

"Have you got... um, ... a girlfriend?"

"Sort of..."

It feels odd. Peter was your age just two months ago, now he's five years older and likes girls. How weird.

Peter leads you away from the clearing towards a huge rocky outcrop, but before you go around the rock, a purple dragon swoops out of the sky and lands in front of you. Its yellow eyes flutter like a bird's as it gently butts Peter in the chest.

He scratches the dragon's head and grins. "Astera, this is my cousin." He gestures for you to put your hand on Astera's head.

Her scales are softer than you expected, and warm.

"Welcome to Dragons' Hold." Her voice thrums in your mind. *"Peter has spoken of you and his family often. He misses you all. Would you like to come for a ride?"*

"Wow, would I ever!" That'll be three dragon rides today. Luckily the weather at Dragons' Hold is sunny and warm, even though it'll soon be dark.

"Come on," says Peter. "Let's go."

Flipping Hans' cloak over your shoulders to keep it out of the way, you climb up onto Astera's saddle behind Peter. The dragon's huge legs bunch then spring high in the air, her wings flapping to power her ascent. She soars over fruit trees, roaring, startling workers returning from the orchard.

Laughing, Peter pats her side. "She's still young and a little playful. Hold on!"

Astera swoops low over a field then leap frogs up and down. Peter whoops with glee, and you hang on, laughing. This is much more fun than the ride you just had on Handel in the storm. After a while, Astera climbs above a forest until she's high above the lake.

In mid air, she twists her body, so she's head down.

White-knuckled, arms around Peter, you grip his belt as Astera plummets headlong towards the lake. Her wings are tucked against her body and her tail streams out behind her. Your stomach drops. Tears stream from your eyes. Is Peter's mad dragon going to dive into the lake?

The setting sun reflects pink and orange on the water. Astera's reflection looms, a purple blob on the lake's surface that grows bigger by the minute. Heart pounding, you take a deep breath. Then Astera's wings flip out, breaking her descent and she slaps her tail down on the lake, sending a fine spray over you and Peter.

You feel Peter's ribs shaking. He's laughing! You slap his back, playfully. "That was a prank? You're mad!" Shaking your head, you have to admit it was a brilliant one.

Astera flies along the lake's surface, skimming the water with her talons. Roaring, she flips something silver from the lake with her talons, then swoops to catch it in her mouth.

"She's fishing," calls Peter.

Soon you're sitting by the lakeside, eating fish roasted by dragon fire, succulent juice running down your chin.

"This is the best thing I've ever tasted."

"Yeah, well I still miss Dad's cooking." Peter stares into the distance. "And chocolate."

"I have just the thing for you!"

"You haven't, have you?" His eyes fly wide open in

anticipation.

You pull a chocolate bar out of your backpack.

Inhaling the scent, Peter groans and takes a bite. "This is awesome. Absolutely awesome," he says between mouthfuls.

You grin. "So is Astera's fish."

The dragon rumbles and nudges you with her nose, pulling her lips off her teeth, reminding you of a chimpanzee.

"Was that a dragon smile?"

"Sure was." Peter jumps to his feet. "We need to get back before the sun is gone, or Hans will send the dragon patrol out for us. Come on."

A while later, on dragon back, flying over the gravel clearing where you first landed, Peter turns his head to talk to you. "Although I love it here, I really do miss my family," he says. "Sometimes, I wish there was a way to go home."

You shrug. "I just assumed a dragon could open a portal when I needed it."

"I've never seen a portal again." Peter looks so sad. For a moment you wonder if either of you are ever going to see your families again. "You know, I wish—" Peter breaks off, pointing beyond Astera's head. "Look!"

A shimmering oval of swirling colors is right in front of you, barely visible against the sunset.

Peter turns to you. "I'm going. Want to come home?"

126

It is time to make a decision. Do you:
Go home with Peter? **P181**
Or
Stay at Dragons' Hold? **P184**

You have decided to take the raft and go down the river.

You grab the pole and stride onto the jetty. It groans and creaks. A piece of rotten wood gives way. You crash onto the raft. Water splashes over the side, submerging one end. It looks dangerous, so you grab the tether rope to haul yourself back to the jetty. The rope rips free and you're adrift. Water seeps into your sneakers.

The edge of the river is slower moving, and you feel like a little adventure – after all it's not every day you travel through a portal into another world, and what could be worse than the trip you just took in the dragon's clutches?

Shoving hard with the pole, you push the raft out towards the centre of the river. You're not used to rafting, so your arms tire quickly. You relax and let the river do the hard work. Sitting on your backpack to avoid getting wet, you watch the forest and farms go by. Hungry, you reach into the pocket of your backpack for a sandwich and realize that your food is wet. Oh well, at least you can munch on chocolate and enjoy the scenery.

Ahead, the river narrows as the banks rise. The current snatches your raft and you start to move swiftly. That's easy to fix. You leap up and grab the pole, upsetting the raft slightly and letting more water on board. Plunging the pole into the water to slow the raft, you nearly fall off when the pole hits nothing. The water is too deep! You overbalance, stumbling to your knees. The pole floats away down the river.

The banks get higher, becoming steep cliffs on either side. The water rushes through a narrow channel, foaming and white where it hits jagged rocks. You have no choice but to cling to the raft through the surging water. About now, you wish another dragon would pluck you into the air.

Twice you are submerged, but your trusty raft pops back to the surface with you hanging tight. The cliffs open out and the river widens into a smooth-flowing broad expanse of water with a forest on one side and fields on the other.

Glad the rough part of your trip is over, you lie on the soggy raft, with even soggier clothing, hoping the sun will dry you out. Knuckles scraped and exhausted after your ordeal, you drift to sleep.

And awaken to an odd roaring noise. Your raft is still floating – barely. It's an inch or two under water and your back and legs are really wet. Cocking an ear, you listen. What's that roaring?

Heart pounding, you figure it out. It's a waterfall. The current picks up. The raft speeds along, far from the banks. You round a corner. And face churning white froth broken by dangerous rocks.

If only you had your pole, you could steer. Helpless,

you hang on to the raft. It careens into a rock, splintering to pieces. Your chest slams into the rock, knocking the air out of you. Pushed under churning white water, you struggle to the surface, clinging to a piece of wood. Water hits your face, entering your mouth and stinging your eyes. You're swept over the edge of the falls.

The roar hurts your ears. Your belly drops. Pieces of raft debris slam into you. You cling to the wood, falling, still falling. It seems to take forever to get down the falls. Then, through the spray you see shimmering colors and wonder... could it be? It is!

A portal. It's a portal!

To reach it, you'd have to twist your body and let go of the wood. But if you hold onto the wood, you may be able to ride down the falls and have something to float on when you hit the bottom.

It is time to make a decision. Do you:

Hold the wood and ride down the falls? **P190**

Or

Dive through the portal? **P192**

You have decided to face the tharuks.

"I'm staying," you say, "even if it's alone."

"Rather you than me," says Bart, and jumps into the wagon. Bax and Becks squeeze in after him.

"On second thoughts, I think you'll be fine on your own," Wil says nervously, jumping in the wagon too. "I'm sorry, Zeebongi. Good luck."

Aria wraps her tail around your neck and nuzzles your face. *"Thank you for helping me, but I need to get back to my mother."* Jumping into the wagon, she snuggles up to Wil.

Giant John shakes his head. "Are you sure?"

You nod.

He slams the side of the wagon shut and leaps onto the seat. Snapping the reigns, he drives out the gate, leaving you alone.

Tharuks race into the stable yards, tusks dribbling dark saliva and red eyes gleaming. Their roaring stops. The stench of rotten flesh wafts on the breeze. Silently, they surround you, their claws at the ready. You gulp.

"Where's that delicious baby dragon?" barks one. "I know you had it."

"I d-don't know what you're talking about, I'm j-just a stable hand," you stutter.

"If we can't have dragonet dinner, we'll settle for stable hand stew," says another.

They laugh menacingly and close in.

Sorry, this part of your story is over. Staying to fight a troop of monsters when Giant John could have helped you to escape, may not have been the best choice. It's not too late, you can go back to your last decision and choose to go with Giant John.

Other adventures are waiting. You could go to Horseshoe Bend, be snatched by a dragon, train as a wizard, or find out what happens when you feed tharuks chocolate.

It is time to make a decision. Do you:
Go back to your last choice and choose differently, to see what happens? **P80**
Or
Go to the list of choices and start reading from another part of the story? **P206**
Or
Go back to the beginning and try another path? **P1**

You have decided to follow Bax and Becks home.

"Wil, Aria, I hope you understand, I have to go back to my world." You shake hands with Wil.

Aria leaps on your shoulder and licks your face. You laugh.

"I'll come with you, just for a moment." says Aria, *"Jump."*

You leap through the portal, Aria's tail wrapped tightly around your neck, and land on the grass in the park next to school. Bax and Becks are standing nearby. Opening the last can of chili tuna fish, you feed it to Aria.

A moment later, Bart lands on the grass. His clothing is tattered and torn. Bax and Becks gape at Bart.

"We thought you were dog food!" says Bax. "Glad you're back!"

"Just escaped," says Bart, "but the wolves shredded my clothes." He gestures at his torn shirt and ripped jeans.

Becks points at you. "It's your fault," she says. "You set the wolves on him. That boy told us so."

You smile. "This is Aria," you say. "She's my friend too, just like those wolves. And she'll be coming to visit me often."

"Now?" asks Aria in your mind.

You nod. Aria leaps into the air, and opens her tiny maw. A blast of fire shoots past the Thomson twins, not harming anyone, but it's enough to send them running.

Aria snorts. You laugh.

"Goodbye, Zeebongi!" says Aria, snorting again. *"What a ridiculous name Wil gave you. I like your real one much better. Thank you for helping me to find my mother. I'll see you soon."*

"Bye, my friend." You wave.

With a flip of her tail, Aria dives back through the portal.

Only a few minutes have passed since you left. In the distance the bus motor is still running. Racing across the field, you are the last one aboard. The only spare seats are down the back - with the Thomson twins.

Everyone looks at you sympathetically, expecting you'll have to stand all the way.

"We saved you a seat," Bart calls out.

"We told them to wait," Becks adds, as you plop down next to Bax. There's shocked silence from the other students as the twins chat to you about how to beat wolves and how high you'd need to fly before there was no air to breathe.

The school picnic is great. The Thomson twins are kind to everyone all day, although you have to laugh when the teacher gives them a detention. She says they smell of smoke and won't believe them when they say they've never touched a cigarette in their lives. From that day on, they treat you respectfully.

Congratulations, you have rescued a baby dragonet

and reunited her with her mother, outwitted wolves and made a happy truce with the Thomson twins. Now and then, Aria creates a portal allowing you back into Dragons' Realm so you can have more adventures.

There are many other adventures in Dragons' Realm. Perhaps you'll be snatched by a dragon, raft down a waterfall, train as a wizard, or face tharuks – the dangerous monsters in the forests of Dragons' Realm.

It is time to make a decision. Do you:
Go to the list of choices and start reading from another part of the story? **P206**
Or
Go back to the beginning and try another path? **P1**

You have decided to feed Aria chili tuna fish so she can flame the wolves

The tree thuds as a wolf slams into the trunk, trying to shake you out. The other wolves copy it, slamming against the tree. Your branch wiggles with each thud.

Legs clinging to the branch, you tear the can of chili tuna fish open. Aria gulps it and zips into the air, swooping down to blast a wolf with a jet of flame. It yelps and scampers off into the forest, its ears flat and tail between its hind legs.

Aria roars. Her purple body hurtles through the air towards another wolf, shooting flames at its face. Howling, it takes off into the trees. Another stubborn wolf is still leaping up at the tree, snapping. Whirling in midair, Aria swoops under a branch and flames its chest. The wolf lunges at Aria and grabs her tail in its jaws.

Aria's whine of pain slices through you.

Breaking off a branch, you drop it on the wolf's head. It growls, jaws flying open, and Aria scorches its nose, sending it scurrying. You snap off more branches, flinging them at the frenzied wolves. "Get out of here, you overgrown doggies," you yell. "Go and bother someone else."

Will applauds. "Go, Zeebongi! Scare those mangy mutts."

Breathing fire, zipping in and out among the wolves,

Aria scares the rest away.

"Zeebongi! Aria! You are my absolute heroes!" Wil exclaims.

Aria's flames splutter and die.

Two people in modern clothing rush into the clearing, panting and gasping. Swinging out of the tree, you and Wil jump down to greet Bax and Becks.

"It's you two," you say, taken aback. "Wil, these are the Thomson twins."

Bax shakes his head. "We're not twins any more. There are only two of us now."

Wil nudges you, speaking softly. "Everyone knows two means twins. Even I can count better than them."

"We know that, but they don't!" you whisper, smiling at Wil. Then you ask Bax, "What happened to Bart?"

"He was eaten by an angry burned wolf." Becks leans against Bax, sobbing.

He puts his arm around her. "It's alright, Becks. Now he won't force us into bullying Fart-face anymore. Or anyone else."

Her face brightens. "That's true. I wasn't worried about Bart though. It's just that I got my best boots dirty!"

Bax laughs. "They'll scrub up fine."

"Why don't you come with us to Dragons' Hold?" Wil asks. "And train as dragon riders."

"Dragons?" Bax grins. "That would be cool!"

"Cold?" asks Wil. "I don't understand."

"It means he'll come," you explain. "Let's get to the blue guards."

A fierce downdraught rustles the leaves above you. Enormous blue and purple wings circle above the treetops.

"It's the blue guards," Wil says.

"And my mother!" calls Aria.

"Follow them," you shout.

Aria bursts into song. Bax and Becks clamp their hands over their ears to drown out Aria's singing. Racing after the flying dragons, you come to a clearing. The blue dragons land, tucking their magnificent wings against their bodies. A purple dragon trumpets and lands beside them.

Aria hurtles towards the purple dragon, shrieking at the top of her voice. Her mother sings too, her deep voice blending with Aria's to create a gorgeous harmony.

"That's beautiful," you murmur, surprised they sound so good together.

"Meet my mother," Aria says in your mind.

"Thank you for finding Aria," the female rider on the purple dragon calls. "We've been hunting for her everywhere. When we heard wolves were in the area, we came to check."

"You're welcome," says Wil, "but it was the Great Zeebongi who found Aria." He gestures at you.

"Zeebongi!" The rider smiles. "We'd like to invite you to Dragons' Hold so you can be Aria's rider when she's big enough."

You're so thrilled, you can't speak. Aria zips around, turning somersaults in excitement.

Wil answers for you. "That would be magnificent, but I'm afraid the Great Zeebongi will need all of us to come."

The dragon rider laughs, "Of course."

Bax and Becks frown and mouth *Zeebongi?* at each other, then shrug. You climb into the saddle behind the woman riding Aria's mother, admiring the dragon's glowing scales. Wil, Bax and Becks grin at you from their seats behind the blue guards.

Aria dives into her saddlebag, then pokes her nose out cheekily. *"I'm so glad you'll be my rider."*

"So am I," you say, grinning like an actor in a toothpaste commercial.

Congratulations, you have rescued a baby dragonet and reunited her with her mother. You have also outwitted vicious wolves and have no problems with Bax and Becks anymore. Aria grows at a rapid rate, and soon you are riding her. Now and then, she creates a portal so you can visit your family, always surprised at how little time has passed on earth. There are still many more adventures in Dragons' Realm.

If you choose again, you could face tharuks – the dangerous monsters in Dragons' Realm – imprint with your own dragon, or train as a wizard or dragon acrobat.

It is time to make a decision. Do you:
Go to the list of choices and start reading from another part of the story? **P206**
Or
Go back to the beginning and try another path? **P1**

You have decided to farewell Aria and return home.

"I have to return to my family," you say, "or they'll be worried."

Wil hugs you. "Zeebongi, thank you for bringing me to Dragons' Realm. You're so clever. I'll always remember how you fed Aria the pepper fish so she could flame that tharuk. You're so wise."

You try not to wrinkle your nose – he still stinks of horse manure. Now that you're saying goodbye, Wil's compliments don't bother you so much. "Thanks, Wil. Have fun riding dragons."

Aria's mother lowers her head to your height. Her purple scales gleam in the early evening sun. You touch her head and her voice rumbles through your mind. *"You have my undying gratitude for returning my daughter. At last I can hear her sweet songs again."*

You smile. Aria's songs aren't exactly sweet, but that's okay with you.

A bundle of scales, energy and tail flaps into your chest, nearly bowling you over. You fling your arms around Aria, hugging her goodbye.

"Don't worry," she says, *"I won't tell Wil your name isn't really Zeebongi."*

"Thank you." You nuzzle against her. "I'm going to miss you."

Nearby, Bax sniffs. "It's sad to leave these dragons," he says.

Aria leaps out of your arms to her mother with a roar. *"Don't worry,"* she says. *"I'll make more world gates. You'll be back to visit in no time."*

The air in front of you shimmers. The twins leap through the portal. You swallow a lump in your throat, wave to Aria and Wil and dive through.

You land on the grass at the front of the school. The bus for the picnic is there and kids are just getting on board. It's like almost no time has passed. The Thomson twins are sprawled nearby.

"Phew, Bart," says Becks, waving her hand in front of her nose. "You still stink of horse poo."

"Who cares?" says Bart. He turns to you. "Hey, that was awesome!"

"Let's get to the picnic," says Bax.

You all race for the bus. Once on board, the teacher keeps checking everyone's shoes for poo, and when they all turn up clean, can't understand where the smell of dung is coming from.

At the picnic, your friends can't figure out how you made friends with the Thomson twins, and ask you, "Why do the Thomson twins call you the Great Zeebongi?"

"It's because Highly-esteemed Zeebongi the Magnificent is too tricky to pronounce!"

The Thomson twins laugh, and Bart says to your friends, "By the way, can't you count? We're not twins, we're triplets!"

You never have a problem with the Thomsons again. In fact, they stop bullying people, and you become friends, visiting Dragons' Realm together whenever Aria creates a portal.

Congratulations, this part of your story is over. You have reunited a dragonet with its mother and become a hero, escaped from tharuks and made friends with the Thomson twins.

You could also train as a wizard, give ravenous wolves earache, test the strongwood trees, or find out what happens when you feed tharuks chocolate.

It is time to make a decision. Do you:
Go to the list of choices and start reading from another part of the story? **P206**
Or
Go back to the beginning and try another path? **P1**

You have decided to stay with Mickel.

"Hans, thank you for your offer, but I think I'll stay here with Mickel."

"I wish you many happy landings," says Hans, clapping you on the shoulder. He climbs upon Handel. The dragon flexes his powerful back legs and lifts off into the sky, his bronze scales shining in the sun.

Mickel takes you back to the forge and shows you how to operate the bellows to keep the coals in the fire glowing.

You pump the bellows, knowing the exercise will keep up your strength. You effortlessly lift a heavy sword from the fire and hold it still, while Mickel hammers it under Sturm's supervision.

Sturm shows you how to hammer out the metal blade of a spade. Your newly-developed muscles let you swing the heavy blacksmith's hammer with ease. It's obvious that Mickel's daily routine will help you stay in shape.

At the end of the day, after a fine dinner of fresh bread and vegetable soup, you fall, exhausted, into your new bed – a hard mattress stuffed with straw, on a rickety wooden frame.

After a few days, you're lifting toddlers above your head, as they shriek with delight, queuing to have a turn. A while later you're lifting bigger kids and easily helping

Mickel with his heaviest duties.

By the end of the first week, you can fling the pigs back into the sty whenever they charge you. The wee porkers squeal with delight. They'd only been hoping to play! Life is fun at Horseshoe Bend settlement.

One day while you're out for your training run with Mickel, the air near you starts to shimmer. You've seen this once before – it's a world gate! It's been so long since you saw your family and friends.

Mickel gasps. "It's beautiful. Look at all those spinning colors."

"Mickel." You clear your throat. "I have to go home. You'll always be my best friend, but I miss my family and my own bed."

Mickel nods sadly.

"Travel well, my friend. Good luck."

"Thank you, Mickel. You can have my rucksack and the things inside it, and you can have these too." Pulling off your sneakers, you pass them to him. He may as well use them on his runs. Going barefoot through these forests has to suck.

He hugs the shoes.

With a lump in your throat, you jump through the portal and land on the neatly-mown grass of the park next to school.

A bus is rumbling in the distance. The twins are exactly where you left them – it's like no time has passed at all.

"Oi, Fart-face!" Bart Thomson yells.

Standing straight, you face the three of them. Their eyes rove over you. "Yeah, what do you lot want?" You feel strong and confident – for the first time in years.

"Um…" Bart stares at your strong arms. "Um, the teacher wanted us to find you."

"Yeah," mumbles Becks. "Hope that's okay."

"What happened to your shoes?" Bax asks.

"Don't need them," you answer. "Tough feet."

"Tough everything," mutters Bart to Becks and Bax. "How did that happen so fast?"

Becks and Bax shrug.

You smile and sprint to the bus, leaving them to eat your dust.

Congratulations, you have had a ride on a dragon, grown very strong, and the Thomson twins won't be bothering you any time soon. There are many more adventures. Maybe you'd like to visit Dragons' Hold, train as a wizard, raft down a waterfall, or find a lost dragonet.

It is time to make a decision. Do you:

Go to the list of choices and start reading from another part of the story? **P206**

Or

Go back to the beginning and try another path? **P1**

You have decided to stay in the tree.

Two tharuks leap up and grab the base of your branch, shaking it so violently that your jaw rattles in your skull. Roaring, they climb the tree.

Mia yowls as a tharuk slashes at the net. "You got me, you brute." She spurts a flame at the beast who backs off, then runs and leaps up, swinging itself onto your branch.

The three tharuks swarm along the tree towards you, two on the trunk below, one on the branch in front of you.

The air just below you shimmers, giving you an idea.

Diving into the portal, you hear Mia scream, "No, don't leave me!"

You land in the park on the lawn.

The Thomson twins run towards you. Bart hollers, "Let's get Fart-face."

"Can't catch me," you call, diving back through the portal.

Bart bellows and follows you through, landing on the ground beside you. Becks and Bax thud to the ground too.

A tharuk roars and charges.

"Yay," yells Bart. "Fist fight!" He swings into action, punching the monster on the nose.

It howls and takes off.

Becks trips another, then leaps on its back, tugging on

his tender ears.

The beast flees into the forest, whimpering. Bax and Bart gang up, attacking the last tharuk together. You and Mia help, flames flying from your fingers.

The remaining tharuk pleads for mercy, "Please, please, just let me go. I'll never bother humans again."

As the beast runs into the forest, you shoot flames at the ropes suspending Mia's net from the tree. The net lands on the ground, and Mia struggles out of it, snatching up her bow and training it on the Thomson twins.

"You could've caught me," she says, "instead of letting me fall."

Bart, Becks and Bax glance at the sparks trailing from your fingers, then at Mia's bow.

"Um, all good, now, right?" asks Bart. "I mean, we did come and help you...," he says lamely.

You frown. "We'll see what the Master Wizard has to say." But inside you're smiling. The Thomson twins won't be bothering you again.

Congratulations, you have harnessed environmental magic, frightened away the tharuks and shown the Thomson twins that you won't be bullied again.

If you choose again you could ride a dragon, rescue a lost dragonet, encounter wolves or make it back home again.

It is time to make a decision. Do you:

Go to the list of choices and start reading from another part of the story? **P206**

Or

Go back to the beginning and try another path? **P1**

You have decided to dash into the forest.

Upset that Mia has been using you for target practice, you dash into the forest – thrashing through ferns and undergrowth, and running between the trees – anywhere to get away from Mia's stupid arrows. She's so infuriating. She scared the pants off you. What an arrow-flinging, arrogant, unbearable–

What was that?

A snort! From the trees ahead. A gray-furred creature breaks through the ferns, looming in front of you. It walks on two legs and is dressed like a warrior. Its beady red eyes gleam and dark saliva runs down its stubby tusks. The stench of rotten meat wafts on the breeze, making you gag. More of the creatures step out from behind trees. Soon you're surrounded. The beasts start to growl, their claws extending and retracting.

The ferns and trees all look the same. Which direction did you come from? Your knees tremble. Why did you run off in a strange world without anyone to guide you?

Reaching into your pocket, you grasp Master Giddi's knife, but it's too small. It'll be useless against those beasts with their long cruel claws.

And you can't even harness any magic, because you didn't finish your lessons. Or can you? Raising your palms, you desperately try to summon a flash shield, a flame, a spark.

Nothing happens.

Snarling, the monsters close in, bringing the foul stink closer. Your stomach churns. You are about to die. Anything would have been better than this – even Mia's tree-hugging lessons. Even being pierced by one of her arrows. Even those giant spiders.

The monsters' snarls are the last thing you hear.

I'm sorry, this part of your story is over. Running off into the forest in a strange new world without paying any attention to where you were going, without learning magic and without a guide, was not the best choice. But don't worry, you can try again.

On your next adventure, perhaps you will be snatched by a dragon, encounter wolves, become a dragon acrobat or create chaos at the marketplace in Montanara.

It is time to make a decision. Do you:

Go back to your last choice and stay with Mia, to see what happens? **P39**

Or

Go to the list of choices and start reading from another part of the story? **P206**

Or

Go back to the beginning and try another path? **P1**

You have decided to go with Wil and Aria to Dragons' Hold.

"I'd love to come to Dragons' Hold." You grin from ear to ear. "Wil says it's where dragons and riders live."

Aria leaps into one of her mother's saddlebags, then pops her head up with her snout sticking out. You and Wil swing up into the saddle. Within moments, you're airborne, the breeze rushing through your hair. Aria's mother's scales gleam in the sun. Atop her back you get a good look at the dragon's wings. Strong and ridged, they're nearly translucent in places, her muscles moving effortlessly to keep you in the air.

The trees are a vast tapestry of greens below you, leaves rustling in the downdraughts from the dragon's wingbeats as you pass. Mountains rise before you, with glistening snow-capped peaks above rocky faces. From so high, the world is silent, except for Wil's breathing, his excited gasps behind you – and the dragon's rhythmic flapping.

Thin trails of smoke rise from isolated cottages among the trees.

"Zeebongi," whispers Wil. "This is incredible. I can see for miles."

"Imagine riding a dragon every day," you reply.

"That's what I've always wanted to do," says Wil. "I've been training in archery for years. Shooting from dragon back will be challenging, but I'm keen to try."

Aria's mother climbs high along the steep mountain faces.

"Those are Dragon's Teeth," says Aria, *"sharp and pointy, just like mine."* She opens her maw to show you her fangs.

As you pop over the top of the mountain range, you can see why they're called Dragon's Teeth. The jagged peaks form a ring. Inside is a valley. Dragons fill the air, riders astride their backs.

"Home. We're home!" Aria sings, and her mother joins in. Somehow her mother's deep voice balances Aria's voice, the notes no longer jangling, but flowing over you in harmony.

Near you, a blue dragon trumpets. Bart is hanging onto the rider's back, his clothing in tatters.

Aria's mother roars in response and lands on the edge of a silver lake, edged by forest. Several other dragons alight nearby, their riders jumping down to meet you. Bart hangs back, watching.

It's like a home coming, with riders cheering and dragons roaring.

"Thank you for saving Aria."

"You saved our dragonet."

"She's home!"

"You hear us, you hear us."

"Zeebongi hears us!"

You think your mind will burst, so many voices sound

in your head at once.

"The dragons say that I hear them. What does that mean?" you ask Wil.

"It's part of the prophecy. Zeebongi is the only one who can hear all the dragons. Most people can't hear any dragons at all, and riders only hear their own dragons, but you're special." He beams. "And you also rescued a dragonet – tharuk monsters often kill dragon babies or even eat them!"

A beautiful dragon strides towards you, every scale gleaming with the colors of the rainbow. Around you, riders bow. Wil falls to his knees with a look of awe on his face. You bow too. A regal-looking rider swings out of the saddle.

"My name is Anakisha," she says. "Rider of Zaarusha, the Dragon Queen of Dragons' Realm."

Zaarusha, the majestic dragon, bumps your shoulder with her snout. *"Thank you for saving Aria."*

"Zaarusha and I will grant you anything you want," says Anakisha. "What gift would you like, Zeebongi?"

"Name it. Name it," say the dragons.

"My friend Wil has a dream," you say. "Could he be a dragon rider?"

A smaller blue dragon comes forward and bows before Wil. He puts out his hand to touch her and you hear what he hears. *"Hello Wil, I'm Wilhemena, the dragon you were born to fly with."*

Grinning, Wil hugs her. For the first time since you've known him, he's speechless.

You sigh, happy that Wil's dream has come true. You would enjoy it here too, if you didn't miss your family so much. "There's something else I'd like," you say.

"Whatever you want," Anakisha replies.

You point at Bart who is skulking around the edge of the crowd, glowering at you. "Bart was attacked by wolves. He needs new clothes and has to get home."

Bart's eyes fly wide open and he gapes at you. A rider passes him a tunic and trousers, and he ducks behind a dragon to get changed. When he reappears he claps you on the shoulder. "Thanks, buddy."

Bart has never, ever called anyone *buddy*. You nod. "No problem."

Zaarusha's voice rumbles through your mind. *"You've chosen a gift for Wil and Bart, but none for yourself, so we gift you the chance to become Aria's rider."*

Aria somersaults through the air to land on your chest, knocking you to the ground. She licks your face like a dog, then flaps her wings in glee. The air shimmers near you as a portal appears.

Aria's eyes whirl. *"I've opened a portal so you can go home. You'll still hear me from your world and I'll hear you. When I'm older, you can return to be my rider."*

You and Bart tumble through the portal and catch up to Becks and Bax who are running for the bus. The other kids love Bart's new rugged clothes, making him smile, instead of glowering at them like usual. From that day on, the Thomson twins are always on their best behavior, looking out for others, and begging you to take them back to Dragons' Realm. Sometimes you take them on your adventures.

Congratulations, you have become a hero in Dragons Realm, rescued a dragonet and made great new friends. The Thomson twins will never hassle you again, and one day soon, you'll return to ride Aria.

There are many more adventures in Dragons' Realm. You could train as a wizard, learn to wrestle, develop your strength or become a dragon acrobat.

It is time to make a decision. Do you:

Go to the list of choices and start reading from another part of the story? **P206**

Or

Go back to the beginning and try another path? **P1**

You have decided to convince Becks to stay with the tharuks.

"Hey Becks," you say, "you have a real way with those tharuks. How would you like to stay here and be in charge of them?"

"Wow!" She grins. "You mean I'd boss them around all day? And they won't answer me back like my brothers do?"

You nod. "As long as we have enough chocolate."

"Oh that's easy," says Becks. "Hey, Bart, Bax…"

They turn to her, poised by the portal, about to jump through.

"You'll be back in an hour with a suitcase of chocolate!"

Bart wrinkles his nose. "You think we want to come back to this weird place?"

"Yeah, I do." Becks smiles wickedly. "Or Dad will find out Bax smashed the window on his Porsche. And Bart, Mom might just get a mysterious message mentioning who gave Bobby McGraff a broken arm."

Bart nods quickly, "A suitcase of chocolate in an hour? No problem."

"Make that two suitcases," says Bax. "We'll see you soon."

You focus on the energy around you and summon a blast of fire from your hands. "Real soon. Otherwise I'll be through the portal for you in no time."

"So will I," Mia pipes up, firing an arrow that flies with uncanny precision between Bax and Bart.

Bax stares at the arrow quivering in a tree trunk.

Bart gulps. "Back soon," he calls. They jump through the portal.

Becks strokes a tharuk's nose, making it purr, then pats another. "Follow me, my lovelies." She turns to you. "Where to?"

"This way," says Mia.

With your backpack half full of Bart's chocolate, you follow Mia, Becks and the tharuks. Mia leaves arrows in trees so Bart and Bax can find you.

By the time you get to Master Giddi's cottage, Becks has taught the tharuks her favorite boy-band hit. Their throaty voices echo through the forest in discord, but she doesn't seem to care that they're off-tune and out of beat.

"Oooh, baby, yeah, yeah, yeah!"

"Beautiful singing, my lovelies," she croons.

You roll your eyes and follow her into the clearing.

Master Giddi laughs and claps his hands. Their singing stops. "A green-eyed tame tharuk choir?"

"Hypnotized by chocolate," you mutter.

"Makes them submissive," says Mia.

Giddi's bushy eyebrows pull into a frown. "And who is this?"

"I'm boss of the tharuks," says Becks, "and sister of

the chocolate suppliers."

Bart and Bax arrive, puffing, with two heavy suitcases. Bart walks straight into a mesmerized tharuk.

"Oof!" Bart says. "Got your chocolate. Plenty more where that came from."

"I see," says Master Giddi.

Secretly, you're not sure whether he does.

He clears his throat and continues speaking, "Well, it's good that you're here. I need some junior apprentices to serve under these two." He waves a hand towards you and Mia. "And make sure you do what they say, or I might just turn you into a tharuk."

Bart and Bax stare at the furry creatures sitting at Becks' feet and gulp.

You grin. Master Giddi does understand, after all.

Congratulations, you have harnessed environmental magic, tamed the tharuks and solved your problems with the Thomson twins. Perhaps you'd also like to ride a dragon, learn to wrestle, rescue a dragonet or make it back home again.

It is time to make a decision. Do you:

Go to the list of choices and start reading from another part of the story? **P206**

Or

Go back to the beginning and try another path? **P1**

You have decided to use magic so Bart and Bax bring you chocolate.

Mia's eyes gleam as if she understands what you're about to do. She lifts her bow and points an arrow straight at Becks.

Raising your hands in the air, you summon a flash of fire, sending it flickering towards Bart and Bax. They leap back, eyes wide. Bart's hands are shaking and Bax's forehead beads with sweat. They flinch when you raise your hands again.

"Ok, you two. We have your sister hostage. You need to bring us back chocolate. Boxes full of it – if you want to see your sister alive."

"And what if we don't care whether we see her alive again?" Bart sneers.

Bax kicks him. "Ow!" And again. "Ow!" Bart holds his sore shin, hopping on the other foot and glaring at Bax.

Sparks drip from your hands as you approach them. "Oh, I'm sure you want to see your sister again, don't you?"

Becks pipes up. "Of course they do, or Mom and Dad might just find out about–"

Bart's face pales. "No problem. No problem at all. Five boxes of chocolate, is it?"

Five is way more than you expected. You tilt your head, as if their offer is stingy. "Make it six."

"Sure," says Bax. "Come on, Bart." They dive through the portal.

Mia giggles and puts her bow down.

Becks glowers at her. "Honestly, you didn't have to do that! I would've blackmailed them anyway." She absent-mindedly pats the arm of the tharuk standing next to her.

"But that was way more fun!" Mia laughs. "I'd do it again any day." Her laughter fades as a spider lands on her arm. Dropping the bow, she freezes, letting out a strangled cry.

Becks, too, has gone pale.

Laughing, you flick it away. It might come in handy knowing these two tough girls have the same weakness. A moment later, the air shimmers. Bax lands, clutching an empty carton, his mouth covered in chocolate stains.

"Um, sorry," he says, "couldn't resist. Peppermint is my favorite."

Next to Becks, a tharuk starts to get restless. Is the chocolate wearing off?

Becks pulls a cell phone out of her pocket and looks at Bax. You're not even sure if it will work between worlds, but you keep quiet.

"Mom or Dad?" she says, "Your choice."

"I'll be right back!" Bax leaps back through the portal. More tharuks start to stir. Some of them growl, deep in their throats.

"Hurry," you yell.

You duck as heavy cartons fly out of the portal, just missing Mia and Becks. Bart lands on the ground, grinning. "Chocolate for everyone," he calls. "Where's Bax?"

"The rotter ate the lot," Becks sneers, "but I fixed him." She waves up her cell phone. "And you'll keep bringing my lovely tharuks more chocolate every week, please, or Mom will be hearing about—"

"Sure, back soon with more," says Bart, leaping back through the portal as Bax passes him landing with a full box.

Becks grins at you and says, "That should keep them out of trouble."

Congratulations, you have harnessed environmental magic, tamed the tharuks and solved your problems with the Thomson twins.

Eventually Bart and Bax figure out how to bring cocoa beans, palm seeds and sugar cane into Dragons' Realm. Master Giddi plants and harvests them and makes chocolate, keeping the tharuks under control. Becks sets up an earth-style café serving tharuks chocolate and teaching them circus tricks to keep the locals entertained. You become an excellent wizard and never need to be worried about being bullied, ever again.

Maybe you'd also like to ride a dragon, find a dragonet, develop your strength, or go back home again.

It is time to make a decision. Do you:
Go to the list of choices and start reading from
another part of the story? **P206**
Or
Go back to the beginning and try another path? **P1**

You have decided to take Mia through the portal.

You grab Mia's hand. "Come on," you yell, as the tharuks slash her cloak with their sharp claws, leaving it in tatters.

Another tharuk swipes at her head, but misses as you pull her to safety. Yanking Mia, you dive head-first through the portal.

"Oof!" You land face-first on the neatly-mown grass of the park near school.

Beside you, Mia lands nimbly on her feet.

Familiar voices holler, "Hey, Fart-face," and "Oi, you."

Not the Thomson twins! You thought you were rid of them. As you scramble to your feet, something zips past your ear. It's one of Mia's arrows.

Thwack! The hood of Bart's sweatshirt is pinned to a tree trunk by the arrow. Mia trains her bow on Bax and Becks. They hover near Bart, faces pale.

You raise an eyebrow at her. "Nice work."

She grins. "No one calls my friend Fart-face."

"Plee-ese, let us go," Becks whines.

"Quiet," says Mia, gesturing with her bow, "unless you want your nose pierced."

You grin, happy her arrows are no longer trained on you. Holding your hands high, you let sparks fly from your fingertips. The twins' eyes grow as huge as watermelons.

Bart unzips his sweatshirt and wriggles his arms out of

the sleeves, his hood still pinned to the tree. The three of them take off, running.

"No more bullying," you call.

"Of course not," they answer, scampering across the park as fast as they can.

You and Mia laugh. She lowers her bow and places her arrow back in her quiver.

In the distance, a bus starts. You glance at your watch. Only a few earth minutes have passed since you left. "Hey, Mia, how would you like to go on a picnic?"

"What is *picnic*?"

"Trust me. I think you're going to love it." Together you run to catch the bus.

Congratulations, this part of your story is over. You have learned some environmental magic, seen a magnificent bronze dragon, and helped Mia escape from some formidable monsters. It also looks like the Thomson twins won't be bothering you again, and, if they do, a few stray sparks from your fingertips should sort them out.

Maybe you'd like to choose again so you can ride a dragon, discover whether tharuks like chocolate, go white-water rafting or visit Horseshoe Bend. Or perhaps you'd like to start the story over and find out what happens if you hide from the Thomson twins in the trees instead of behind the bleachers.

It is time to make a decision. Do you:
Go to the list of choices and start reading from
another part of the story? **P206**
Or
Go back to the beginning and try another path? **P1**

You have decided to stay and fight the tharuks.

"Remember your lessons," yells Mia.

Tuning into the environment, you hold up your hands and fling flames at the snarling monsters. They bat at their fur and advance. Nocking an arrow, Mia takes aim. Her face turns pale as a hairy spider on a silken thread drops out of a tree in front of her nose. Her legs shake and she drops her bow.

"No, Mia!" you yell. "Focus!"

Holding up a hand, you shoot a blast of flame at the spider, frying it instantly. "Grab your bow," you yell, ducking an angry swipe from tharuk claws.

Whirling, you fling flames at the beasts.

Mia, coming to her senses, snatches up her bow, and fires at a tharuk. It yelps and races into the forest. Her next arrow hits another tharuk's butt as it flees.

Your flames scare the last tharuks into the bushes.

You grin at Mia.

"Not bad," she says. "Not bad at all, for your first day of training." She grins, and you know, when you get home, you'll never have a problem with the Thomson twins again.

Congratulations, this part of your story is over. You have harnessed environmental magic and gained valuable fighting skills that will impress the Thomson twins when you get home.

There are many more adventures in Dragons' Realm. Maybe you could ride a dragon, go white-water rafting, develop your strength, or create chaos in the marketplace at Montanara.

It is time to make a decision. Do you:

Go to the list of choices and start reading from another part of the story? **P206**

Or

Go back to the beginning and try another path? **P1**

You have decided to hide in the marketplace.

"Let's stay here," you say. "Quick, hide." You duck more chicken poo as the birds flap around your head.

Aria dives into a pile of hats, sending them toppling. She buries her head in a floppy red hat, her bottom and tail sticking high in the air.

"Aria, no, we can still see you." You run from a furry brute headed your way.

"Oh? I can't see you," Aria, replies.

Wil snatches Aria up like a football and leaps over a table, racing behind a wagon. You lose sight of them as a tharuk grabs your backpack. Shrugging it off your shoulders, you race away, leaving the monster rummaging through your bag.

Around you, people send livestock running through the square. Traders wave brightly colored fabric to distract them. Through the mayhem, more tharuks march three people into the square – the Thomson twins. They tie them to a wagon on the far side of the marketplace.

Ducking a tharuk and scrambling under a baker's stall, you make your way towards the Thomson twins. Even though they've bullied you and teased you, you can't leave them here with those monsters.

Bart looks up, surprised. "Why are you helping us?"

"You look a bit stuck." You grab a knife off a stand of tools and cut their ropes. "Create as much havoc as you can. We're trying to save the dragonet."

"Sure thing," Bart nods at Bax and Becks. "Come with me, you two." He runs over to a table laden with pastries. "Food fight!" Bart yells, and throws a pie straight into a tharuk's face.

Bax and Becks laugh and join in. Soon there are pies, pastries and cakes flying at the tharuks. People pelt them with vegetables, and someone joins in, throwing horse dung. Roaring in frustration, the beasts group on the far side of the market place.

You sigh in relief. But where are Wil and Aria?

Dashing around the wagon, you find Wil and Aria facing a tharuk. It has your backpack in its hands.

"Sing, Aria! Now!" you shout.

She opens her mouth and screeches. The tharuk claps its hands over its ears and drops your backpack.

Snatching it up, you pull the tab on the can of chili tuna fish and thrust it at Aria. She stops singing, gulping the tuna fish down in one swallow. Flames erupt from her maw and she flies after the tharuk, chasing it out of the square.

Wil grins. "You're so clever, Zeebongi the Magnificent."

Bart, Bax, Becks and the local people are still pelting the other monsters with food, but soon their supplies will run out. You run over to help them, picking up a huge pie and throwing it straight at the troop leader.

In midair, Aria flies at the pie-splattered tharuk leader and shoots a jet of flame at him.

"Fire!" he yells. "Disperse! Back to Commander Zens."

Ear-splitting roars sound above you. An enormous purple dragon is above the square, flanked by blue dragons.

"Mother!" Aria yells.

"The blue guards!" calls Wil, eyes shining.

The tharuks dash from the square, racing down the streets. The blue guards' dragons fly after them, roaring.

"Zeebongi! Zeebongi!" the people shout. You think your ears will pop with all the noise.

Someone rushes over and brings you and Wil chairs. Other folk scramble to give you the last of the pastries and pies.

Bart serves you cake. "Thanks for saving us."

Behind him Becks and Bax echo their thanks too. Becks tries on a hat.

Aria's mother lands nearby. Aria zips through the air, nuzzling her mother and purring like a cat.

"Mother wants to know if you'd like to come to Dragons' Hold with us," Aria says in your mind.

"But my family…"

"Don't worry, I can make a portal for you to visit home, any time you want."

You smile. "Aria, I'd love to stay in Dragons' Realm.

That would be awesome."

Wil hears you. "You're staying? Zeebongi, that's wonderful."

You turn to the Thomson twins. "Do you want to stay here or go?"

Becks grins. "I'd like to learn how to make these crazy hats."

"Go home and leave these delicious pastries behind?" Bart licks his fingers. "No way!"

"I love the dragons," says Bax.

"The blue guards will be back soon. I'm sure they'll take us all to Dragons' Hold, Zeebongi," says Wil.

"There's only one thing." Bart Thomson stares at you intensely. "Go on. Tell Wil your real name."

"Alright," you sigh. "My name is–"

"Zeebongi!" The Thomson twins chorus, interrupting you.

You know you'll never be able to use your real name again!

Congratulations, this part of your story is over. You have reunited a dragonet with its mother and become a hero, escaped from tharuks, and made friends with the Thomson twins.

Your new life at Dragons' Hold is full of adventure and everyone honors you as Zeebongi, even the Thomson twins, who never tell anyone your real name.

Aria and Wil become your best friends. Now and then, you go back through a portal to see your family, amazed at how little time has gone by on Earth. Who knows, maybe one day you'll convince them to come to Dragons' Realm too.

Perhaps you'd like another adventure, training as a wizard, going white-water rafting, or finding out what happens when you feed tharuks chocolate.

It is time to make a decision. Do you:

Go to the list of choices and start reading from another part of the story? **P206**

Or

Go back to the beginning and try another path? **P1**

You have decided to become a dragon acrobat.

Riders crowd around as you climb out of the saddle, patting your back and congratulating you on your stunt jumps. Hans winks at you, and Handel nudges you with his snout.

Marlies comes over to shake your hand, smiling. "Now I can welcome you properly."

The crowd parts as a dragon lands nearby. You are awestruck. This dragon is even more beautiful than Handel and Liesar. It's larger, and each of its scales gleam with all the colors of the rainbow. The dragon's yellow eyes gaze at you. A middle-aged woman grabs a strap and swings out of the saddle, landing nimbly on her feet. Her piercing blue eyes stand out in her tanned face. Those eyes are turned on you as she walks over.

She glances at Hans, and he bows, then kisses her hand.

"Anakisha, Honored Rider of Queen Zaarusha." He introduces you to her.

You shake her hand, unsure what to do.

"You're a fine acrobat in the making." She smiles. "How would you like to become a dragon rider?"

Grinning, you answer, "Would I ever!"

The riders around you cheer. Marlies comes to stand beside you.

Hans puts an arm over your shoulders, and says,

"We'll find you a dragon tomorrow."

Congratulations, this part of your story is over. You have confronted an archer, defended yourself with a magical flash-shield against a wizard, developed your strength and fitness, and performed stunts on a dragon. You absolutely love your own dragon, Zeebo, who is the perfect shade of green. Life at Dragons' Hold is full of adventure and every day you learn new riding stunts, gaining the respect of other dragon riders. Eventually your family join you in Dragons' Realm.

Maybe you'd like another adventure, giving vicious wolves earache, being snatched by a dragon, or feeding a dragonet chocolate.

It is time to make a decision. Do you:

Go to the list of choices and start reading from another part of the story? **P206**

Or

Go back to the beginning and try another path? **P1**

You have decided to go home with the Thomson twins.

You face Mickel and Hans and say, "Thank you for looking after me and being my friends, but my family will be worried, and I miss them." The whirling portal is getting smaller. You don't have long. "I have to go home."

Handel rumbles. "We understand," says Hans. "Good luck."

"Remember to keep exercising," calls Mickel, as you jump through the swirling air. His voice drifts to you faintly. "And show those Thomson twins who's in charge."

You land on the grass in the park next to school. Bart, Becks and Bax are sprawled nearby. Bart jumps up and runs over to you, helping you to your feet.

"Ah, hope you're all right," he says gruffly.

A faint dragon roar floats through the portal. Bart twitches, staring at the shimmering air. When it closes with a pop, he looks relieved.

In the distance the bus motor is running. Hardly any time has passed.

"Come on," says Bart, taking your backpack for you. "Let's get to that picnic."

You all race to the bus together.

At the school picnic, Bart, Becks and Bax organize the

other kids into a queue and get you to wrestle them. The sports teacher cocks an eyebrow, surprised when you win every match, and suggests that you form a school wrestling club.

Bart instantly nominates you as President. You appoint him as secretary and Becks and Bax as your advisors. Bax's squirrel becomes team mascot.

"Where did you learn to wrestle?" asks the teacher. "I've noticed you all use the same techniques."

Becks grins, "From a big family friend."

"Yeah," says Bax, "You could say he's a giant in the wrestling scene."

All the kids think he's joking. They jostle each other to wrestle you.

"Keep to the rules," calls Bart to the kids. "Wait your turn."

"No cheating," says Becks.

"Yeah," laughs Bax, "or I'll get a huge bronze dragon to eat you!"

Everyone laughs. Except Bart. He just looks nervous.

Congratulations you've developed your strength, been on a dragon, and formed a wrestling club with the Thomsons. Now and then, Handel opens a portal, letting you back into Dragons Realm, where Mickel and Giant John teach you more wrestling tricks so you can stay one step ahead of the Thomson twins. Although you don't ever become best friends with Bart, Becks and Bax, you do have an unusual bond due to your adventure. You tutor the Thomson twins in math, causing them to rename themselves the Thomson triplets.

This is the end of this set of choices but there are plenty more. Perhaps you'd like to train as a wizard, feed a dragonet chocolate or meet tharuks – the dangerous monsters lurking in the forests in Dragons Realm.

It is time to make a decision. Do you:

Go to the list of choices and start reading from another part of the story? **P206**

Or

Go back to the beginning and try another path? **P1**

You have decided to ask Handel to take you home.

"Um…" You scrape the toe of your sneaker over the stony ground sheepishly. "Would you mind if I went home? I miss my family."

"Sure," says Hans. "Family is important." He puts his hand on your shoulder. "Would you like to go now?"

"Can I?"

Marlies shakes your hand. Dragon riders wave as you and Hans climb back into Handel's saddle and the great bronze dragon flies into the sky. In front of Handel, a shimmering oval appears in the air. You take one last glance at Dragon's Teeth, the fierce mountains that guard this beautiful valley.

Handel dives through the portal and lands on the grass in the park next to school. The Thomson twins run out of the trees and freeze, staring at Handel with their mouths hanging open. In the distance a bus is starting. Only a few minutes have passed since you left.

"Who are they?" asks Hans.

"The Thomson twins."

Hans frowns. "Don't you mean triplets?"

"Don't tell them," you whisper. "They can't count!"

Hans laughs. "Good luck. I hope to see you again soon."

Handel gives a dragon-y grin and blows a puff of smoke at the Thomsons. Then he and Hans leap through the portal.

Bart stares at the bronze tip of Handel's tail. "W-w-what was th-that?"

The portal closes with a pop.

"What?" You frown, pretending you're puzzled. "Oh, you mean Handel?"

Bart, Bax and Becks nod, their eyes wide.

"Just a friend of mine. He's always hanging around."

"Um, we'd better get to the bus before it leaves for the picnic," Bax says.

"You coming?" asks Becks.

"I can help you with your bag," says Bart.

"I'm fine, thanks," you say, trying not to smile.

You wonder what the teacher is going to say when she sees Handel's parting gift – the Thomson's soot-covered faces. She's never going to believe that a dragon blew smoke at them.

Congratulations, this part of your story is over. You have ridden a magnificent bronze dragon, met a wizard, developed your strength and fitness, and learned some dragon riding stunts. The teacher gives the Thomson twins a detention for playing with fire and warns them that arson is dangerous. They're too scared of Handel to ever trouble you again.

There are more exciting adventures in Dragons' Realm. Perhaps you'd like to tame a dragonet, find out what happens if you hide from the Thomson twins in the trees instead of behind the bleachers, or meet tharuks — the blood-thirsty monsters that roam Dragons' Realm.

It is time to make a decision. Do you:

Go to the list of choices and start reading from another part of the story? **P206**

Or

Go back to the beginning and try another path? **P1**

You have decided to go home with Peter.

It would be good to see your family again. "Yeah, sure. Let's go."

"I'm so glad you're coming with me," Peter calls. "Go, Astera, jump through the world gate!"

The sunset and Dragons' Hold disappear. The icy peaks of Dragon's Teeth are gone. Astera lands on the neatly-mown grass at the park next to school, near the grove of trees and flower beds. It's still morning. In the distance the bus rumbles and the students chatter as they get on board.

Bart, Becks and Bax run out of the trees, and stop dead, staring.

Astera roars. You leap off her back, landing softly on the grass.

"What's that?" asks Becks, staring at Astera.

The purple dragon sends a small blast of flame towards the Thomson twins. They leap back, huddling together.

"I have to see my family and get Astera back before the portal closes," Peter calls.

You know he's right. "Good luck. See you soon."

Astera is a majestic sight flying across the park towards town, her purple scales gleaming in the sun. The twins gape at her speechless. You take off your cape and rain jacket and stow them in your backpack.

As Astera disappears, Bart, Becks and Bax turn to you. Standing tall, you look Bart directly in the eye.

Bart looks you up and down, obviously noticing your strong arms. His cheek twitches. "Um, I… uh… sorry for giving you a hard time this year." He scrapes the toe of his shoe in the grass and stares at his feet.

Becks looks like she'd rather be somewhere else.

Bax holds out a friendly hand so you can shake it. "Um, uh, want to sit next to me on the bus? It's time to go to the picnic."

You glance at your watch. Almost no time has passed since you went through the portal to Dragons' Realm. "Thanks, Bax, but I can manage getting to the bus." Striding away, you grin, reminding yourself to exercise your new muscles regularly as Mickel has taught you. Looking at your hands, you wonder if a little practice will help you to summon another magical flash-shield.

Your grin grows wider as the twins scamper after you, nearly tripping over themselves in an effort to be nice. Maybe you won't need that flash shield, after all.

Congratulations, this part of your story is over. You have confronted an archer, defended yourself with a magical flash-shield against a wizard, been dragon riding, developed your strength and fitness, weathered a terrible storm and found your missing cousin. And you won't have any more trouble from the Thomson twins, as long as you keep up the fitness routines Mickel has taught you.

Many more adventures await you. Perhaps you could rescue a dragonet, meet Giant John, go rafting, or train as a wizard.

It is time to make a decision. Do you:

Go to the list of choices and start reading from another part of the story? **P206**

Or

Go back to the beginning and try another path? **P1**

You have decided to stay at Dragons' Hold.

"I'm going to stay here, Peter," you say.

"Then you'll have to jump," calls Peter. "Don't worry, Astera will catch you."

Peter stands in his stirrups to give you space. You gulp and awkwardly hoist a leg over the saddle.

"3, 2, 1, jump!" Peter yells.

Heart pounding, you fling yourself off the dragon. The wind snatches your cloak, and you plummet, feet first, towards the stony ground below. What were you thinking?

You should've chosen to go home. If Astera's not quick, you'll be a human pancake.

"Oof!" The air smacks out of you as strong dragon forelegs grasp you in their talons. Astera deposits you gently on the gravel.

"Good luck!" You wave to Peter.

"You too," comes his faint reply.

Astera's tail disappears through the portal. The shimmering air shrinks and disappears.

"I'm glad you've decided to stay," says a voice behind you.

Whirling, you find Hans, his face glowing in the sunset. Above you, the snow-tipped mountains shine orange and pink.

Hans chuckles. "Peter's been here a long time. It's

good for him to have a visit home." He places his arm across your shoulders. "But your adventure is only beginning. Let's find you a place to sleep and, in the morning, a dragon to ride. Before you know it, your dragon will be your new best buddy."

"A dragon of my own? That's amazing!"

Hans chuckles again. "I thought you'd say that."

Congratulations, this part of your story is over. You have confronted an archer, defended yourself with a magical flash-shield against a wizard, developed your strength and fitness, weathered a terrible storm and sent your missing cousin home.

Your new life at Dragons' Hold is full of adventure and your dragon becomes your best friend. Every day you practice the fitness routines Mickel has taught you. Now and then, you go back through a portal to see your family, amazed at how little time has gone by on Earth. Whenever you see the twins at home, they are always utterly respectful, which makes you smile. Sometimes Peter comes to Dragons' Hold and you race through the skies together. Who knows, maybe one day you'll convince your family to come too.

There are many more adventures. You could encounter ravenous wolves, rescue a dragonet, be snatched by a dragon, start a food fight, or meet Giant John.

It is time to make a decision. Do you:

Go to the list of choices and start reading from another part of the story? **P206**

Or

Go back to the beginning and try another path? **P1**

You have decided to do nothing and let Bart die.

Bart's hands slip. "Please," he calls. "I'll never bully you again. And I'll make Becks and Bax stop too."

You watch him silently. The blue dragon he flew on scrabbles, trying to grip Bart, but rocks obstruct it. It roars. Bart's hands slip.

Someone shoves you aside and drops to the ground, reaching over the ledge. It's Marlies. She grabs one of Bart's hands as the other slips. His weight pulls her forward, but she hangs on tight to his arm with both of her hands. Her body slides towards the cliff edge.

Shocked that she could also die, you realize how foolish you've been and sit on her back, trying to prevent her from slipping. "Becks, Bax, help!"

They race from the back of the cavern. Bax grabs Marlies by the legs. In a flash of silver, Liesar lands on the edge of the ledge.

"A rope. In Liesar's saddlebag," cries Marlies.

Becks grabs the rope, passing Liesar one end. The silver dragon clamps it in her jaws. Becks throws the other end down to Bart. He snatches it with his free hand and braces his legs against the cliff face, then Bart lets go of Marlies to grab the rope with his other hand.

You all scramble back from the edge, and Liesar slowly backs towards the cavern, helping Bart up onto the ledge.

Bart puffs and pants. He glares at you. "You were

going to let me die."

"Is this true?" Marlies asks, her voice sharp.

You nod, staring at your shoes.

Bart glowers and mutters at you through gritted teeth. "Watch your back. I'm going to get you! Every day I'll be there, waiting for my chance."

"Yeah, Fart-face!" Bax says.

"Lousy coward!" yells Becks.

"Enough." Marlies holds up a hand. "The chance to become dragon riders could help the four of you to change your relationship and become friends. But dragon riders must have the highest integrity."

"I'm sorry," you mumble, meeting her piercing gaze. "They've been bullying me for years."

"None of you have shown the maturity needed to overcome your grudges." She takes a deep breath, looking each of you in the eye. "I'm afraid you must all go home. Liesar, create a world gate."

The air in front of you shimmers.

"Goodbye," says Marlies, pushing you through the portal.

You land on the grass in the park next to school. Only a few minutes have passed since you left. In the distance, the bus is rumbling. It's about to leave for the picnic. Scrambling to your feet, you start to run.

A thud sounds behind you, then two more.

"Get Fart-face!" yells Bart.

"Right on," shouts Bax.

Becks lets out a whoop.

Their feet pound behind you. You spurt forward. Although you make it to the bus, the school picnic is miserable. The Thomson twins throw your lunch in the river, put beetles in your backpack, and shove you every time no adults are looking. You apologize profusely, but know that Bart is never going to forgive you.

I'm sorry, this part of your story is over. Choosing to let Bart die means that you will not have a chance to become a dragon rider and that the Thomson twins will bully you for years. But don't worry, you can choose again. More adventures await you.

It is time to make a decision. Do you:

Go back to your last choice and save Bart to see what happens? **P198**

Or

Go back to the park and escape the Thomson twins through the hole in the fence? **P3**

Or

Go to the list of choices and start reading from another part of the story? **P206**

Or

Go back to the beginning and try another path? **P1**

You have decided to hold the wood and ride down the falls.

Clinging onto the wood, you fly down the falls in stinging water, into a deep pool. The force of the water submerges you, turning you over and over until you no longer know which way is up.

As your breath starts to give out, you wonder what would have happened if you hadn't struggled with the dragon or if you'd taken the trail along the river.

The wood you were holding flies towards you, hitting you on the head and everything goes black.

You are never found. Although Bart explains that a dragon was involved, no one ever believes him. But there is a positive ending to this story, because the Thomson twins never bully anyone again.

I'm sorry, this part of your story is over. Struggling with a dragon that came to your aid, taking a derelict raft, and not jumping back through the portal may not have been the best choices, but you can try again.

Perhaps you'd like to create chaos in a marketplace, ride a dragon, feed a dragonet chocolate, or encounter tharuks – the dangerous monsters that prowl the forests of Dragons' Realm.

It is time to make a decision. Do you:

Go back to your last choice and dive through the

portal, to see what happens? **P192**

Or

Decide not to take the raft and explore the riverbank trail instead? **P8**

Or

Go to the list of choices and start reading from another part of the story? **P206**

Or

Go back to the beginning and try another path? **P1**

You have decided to dive through the portal.

You dive away from the spray, through the shimmering air. You land in a flower bed in the park next to school, hair and clothes dripping and water running into your eyes. Sinking back among the flowers, you breathe a sigh of relief. The nightmare is over.

Something soggy squelches beneath your back. Sitting up, you examine the remains of your shredded backpack. There isn't much left, except for the battered straps and a piece of torn fabric hanging off them. Your lunchbox, jacket and water bottle are gone. But you're still wearing your watch. It must've stopped a few minutes after you jumped through the portal.

Oh well, at least you're alive.

"Hey Fart-face!"

Not again. Bart Thomson rushes out of the trees towards you, Bax and Becks on his heels. After facing a dragon and an enormous waterfall, the Thomson twins are nothing. They loom over you.

Becks frowns at the water running down your face. "Crying 'coz we caught you?" she sneers.

"Hey, how did you get so wet?" says Bart.

"Just what I want to know!" says a teacher behind them.

The Thomsons whirl.

"It wasn't us!" cries Bax.

"We don't know what happened!" says Becks

"That's what they all say!" The teacher glares. "Look at that backpack. It's ruined." The teacher takes Bart's backpack off him and passes it to you. "I'm sorry they did this. You can have Bart's lunch. Run to the bus. You don't want to be late for the picnic."

Your watch hasn't stopped at all. Time is just different where you've been.

"We didn't do anything! It was a dragon," says Bart. "I saw it. I swear!"

"Bart Thomson. We've had enough of your bullying. And as for you two...,' says the teacher leading the Thomson twins away.

You rush for the bus. Bart's backpack is heavy. You open it and discover all the snacks and money that Bart has stolen from other kids. When you give everybody their stuff back, they treat you like a hero. The school picnic is fun, but from that day on, you are careful around water, especially in rivers. You often wonder what would've happened if you hadn't wriggled and tried to get out of the dragon's grasp. Perhaps you would have had a completely different adventure altogether.

Congratulations, you made it back from Dragons' Realm alive. Your school mates think you're awesome for recovering their stuff. You survived the dragon carrying you in its talons and a crazy trip down a dangerous river on a derelict raft. Perhaps struggling in the dragon's grip may not have been the best decision. Perhaps you would have had a chance to meet dragon riders and ride a dragon yourself, if you hadn't struggled. Taking an old derelict raft from a rotting jetty also may have stopped you from having other exciting adventures.

Many more adventures await you, starting a food fight, giving wolves earache, becoming incredibly strong or rescuing a dragonet.

It is time to make a decision. Do you:

Go back and take the riverbank trail instead of the raft? **P19**

Or

Go back to your last choice and choose differently, to see what happens? **P190**

Or

Go to the list of choices and start reading from another part of the story? **P206**

Or

Go back to the beginning and try another path? **P1**

You have decided to stay at Dragons' Hold and ride Aria.

A crowd of dragon riders come cheering from caves in the mountainside. More dragons land around you, roaring. Their riders clap you and Wil on the back, thanking you for bringing their dragonet home.

"This is the Great Zeebongi," calls Wil.

Around you, the crowd grows still. Then murmurs start.

"A feast," calls a man that looks like a Viking. "Tonight, we'll feast in Zeebongi's honor and to celebrate Aria's return."

The riders cheer. Wil grins. Bart, Bax and Beck whoop too, swept up in the midst of the celebration.

A woman with long dark hair and turquoise eyes approaches you. "Honored Zeebongi, my name is Marlies. I'll train you as a rider until Aria grows." She smiles, making you feel right at home. "And if you need to visit your family, Liesar can take you through a world gate any time you want." She gestures at her dragon.

The silver dragon lowers her head and nudges your shoulder. You stroke her nose. A hum thrums through her body. This is awesome. Yesterday you had no idea dragons existed, now they're your friends.

"Thank you, Marlies, I'd like that."

Wil grabs your arm. "I've always wanted to be a rider,

and now we're here. We made it! I'm so happy."

As Wil starts questioning a dragon rider, Bart approaches you. "Um, thanks. You really aren't so bad after all." He smiles and gives you a friendly elbow in the ribs. "Thanks for bringing us to Dragons' Hold, Fart-face!"

People back home would find your tale of meeting dragons unlikely, but they'd *never* believe Bart Thomson was thanking you.

Your new life at Dragons' Hold is full of adventure and everyone honors you as Zeebongi, even the Thomson twins, who smile but don't tell anyone your real name. Aria and Wil become your best friends. Marlies trains you in archery, sword fighting and riding techniques. Aria grows quickly and is soon large enough for you to ride. You enjoy cruising through the skies on dragon back. Now and then, you go back through a portal to see your family, amazed at how little time has gone by on Earth. Who knows, maybe one day you'll convince them to come to Dragons' Realm too.

Congratulations, this part of your story is over. You have reunited a dragonet with its mother, escaped from tharuks and made friends with the Thomson twins.

More adventures await you. You could train as a wizard, test the strongwood trees, be snatched by a dragon, or find out what happens when you feed tharuks chocolate.

It is time to make a decision. Do you:

Go to the list of choices and start reading from another part of the story? **P206**

Or

Go back to the beginning and try another path? **P1**

You have decided to save Bart.

You can't let Bart die. Lying on the rocky ledge, you reach over the edge and grab Bart's hand, hollering, "I've got you! Hold on!"

Bart's weight drags you forward and your body slips towards the edge of the cliff. The blue dragon roars. Two people thud onto your legs, stopping your slide forward.

"Gotcha!" shouts Bax, calling from your right leg.

"Hang in there, Bart," yells Becks, who's got your other leg.

Behind, the crowd murmurs. Boots appear beside your shoulder, at the edge of the ledge. "Don't worry," Marlies calls to Bart, tossing a rope around him.

Bart braces his feet against the cliff, and uses one hand at a time to get his arms through the rope so it's around his chest. When he's secure, the rope goes taut.

"You alright?" you ask.

Holding the rope, Bart grunts and starts pacing up the cliff face. He's heavy. How is Marlies holding him? Bax and Becks hop off you. You scramble to your feet. Liesar has the rope tight in her jaws, behind Marlies. The silver dragon backs towards the cavern, her powerful leg muscles flexing, hoisting Bart up onto the ledge. Everyone moves out of the way to make room for Liesar's massive body.

Puffing and panting, Bart lies on the ground for a

moment. Becks and Bax haul him to his feet and hug him.

"Man, you're alive!" says Bax.

"Thanks to Fart-face," says Bart, coming over to you. He raises his hand.

You resist the impulse to flinch away. Surely he's not going to hit you.

Bart claps you on the shoulder. "You saved my life. I owe you. We'll never hassle you again." Behind him, Bax and Becks nod. Then Bart hugs you.

It comes as such a shock, you just stand there gaping. "Um, no problem."

"Well done," says Marlies. "Quick thinking is just the type of quality dragon riders need. Take a moment to relax, the dragons will be here soon."

"What dragons?" asks Bax.

Marlies explains, "Those just old enough to imprint. They need riders." She hands you strips of meat. "Once you've imprinted, feed your dragon. It will help establish a bond." Others crowd around her, taking meat too. She and Liesar usher everyone back to the cavern. "Leave space on the ledge for your dragons to land," Marlies says.

Bart puts an arm over your shoulder, and announces loudly. "You're my hero. I hope you get the best dragon."

The crowd murmurs, looking at you in awe.

Confetti-like specks appear in the sky on the other side of the valley. Soon a myriad of colors fill the air and the flurry of wingbeats announces the arrival of the dragons. They land on the ledge.

A pulse of energy thrills through you. Then another. Like a tide, the energy sweeps you forward, until you're eye to eye with a golden dragon. Your heart stands still as she regards you with her startling green eyes. Images and feelings wash through you – her wonder at breaking out of her egg, the thrill of her learning to fly, the joy she feels at meeting you.

A clear high voice sounds in your mind. *"At last, you've come. I've been to the imprinting grounds many times and never met my rider. I'm thrilled you're here. My name is Neronya."* The dragon winks at you. *"Hop on. Come fly with me."*

"Neronya. I can hear your thoughts – that's amazing." Your skin prickles with anticipation. Wonder fills you. She's the most beautiful creature you've ever seen. Her scales glimmer in the sun and her green eyes pierce you, taking your breath away with their intensity. You hold out the strips of meat Marlies gave you. Neronya delicately takes the meat from your hands, then licks your palms clean.

Around you, people and dragons are moving, but you hardly notice them. "You're really choosing me?"

"Of course. You're the only one for me. Dragons choose their riders for life."

Touching the warm scales on her neck, you marvel. Although each scale is tough, her skin is supple and moves under your hand, giving it that soft leather feel. Her scent reminds you of warm summer days outside.

Marlies appears with a saddle, and shows you how to put it onto Neronya's back, then adjust it and fasten the straps.

Impatience grips you. Neronya snorts. You sense she's impatient too. She wants to fly with you. You clamber into the saddle. Her enormous legs tense, and she leaps off the ledge.

Airborne, you let out a whoop. The mountainside falls away. You shoot into the sky. Neronya's golden wings catch the light, shimmering in the sun. Your heart soars as Neronya ascends. Below you, dragons roar, their new riders shrieking with excitement. Neronya bellows in reply, her roar thrumming though her, resonating through your body.

Catching a thermal current, Neronya stops flapping and soars. You glide through the air, adrenaline rushing through you, the wind streaming into your face.

"Yahoo!" you cry.

A ripple of dragon laughter flits through your mind. *"Yahoo is about right, but your yahoos have only just begun."* Neronya furls her wings, tucking them against her side, and dives headfirst towards the valley.

The other dragons are blurs of purple, green, red, blue

and orange as you pass them, plummeting downwards. Snatches of sound whip into your ears, dragons roaring, people calling, but you can't make out their words.

The forest on the valley floor is getting closer. The trees, first a carpet of green, seem to rush up at you, suddenly becoming pointed treetops that could spear you.

"Neronya!" you squeal in panic, thighs tense, and hands tight on the saddle grips.

"*Relax, everything's under control.*" Neronya flips out her wings and breaks your rapid descent, flying over the forest towards a lake.

Your heart slows and you laugh. "That was incredible! Can we do it again?"

Neronya chuckles, a deep throaty sound that vibrates through her. "*I'm glad you enjoyed that. We have plenty of other tricks to try too.*"

"I can't wait!"

A low horn peals throughout the valley.

"*I'm afraid you'll have to wait. We've been summoned.*"

She lands in a grassy clearing near the edge of the lake. A dragon rider with dark curly hair and green eyes, astride a magnificent bronze dragon, much larger than Neronya, blows the horn again.

"*That's Hans,*" says Neronya. "*He trains new riders.*"

Dragons drop out of the sky onto the grass.

Bax is riding a red, Becks is on a green, and Bart has a

purple dragon. They grin and wave at you. Other newly-imprinted riders wave too. Everyone knows you, because they saw you save Bart.

"Liesar mind-melded and showed me how you saved that boy. You'll always be my hero too," says Neronya, raising her head proudly. *"You've saved me from being riderless and given me great joy."*

Your heart swells until you think it will burst. This is much better than a school picnic.

"Who is that boy you saved? And the other two?"

"The Thomson twins," you say. "They used to bully me."

"Even more noble of you to save him, then," Neronya says in your mind, sounding puzzled.

"What is it?" you ask.

"You called them twins, but there are three of them."

"Oh yes, they're actually triplets," you say. "But don't tell them that. They can't count!"

Congratulations, this part of your story is over. You have saved Bart's life, imprinted as a dragon rider and are about to start your training in earnest. Your new life at Dragons' Hold is full of adventure and Neronya becomes your best friend. You know you'd never want to live without her. Bart's experience in falling off the ledge has changed him and he becomes your friend too, never bullying anyone again. Every day, you and the Thomson twins fly through the skies together, enjoying life in Dragons' Realm. Now and then, you go back through a portal to see your family, amazed at how little time has gone by on Earth. Although they miss you, they're thrilled that you're so happy. Who knows, maybe one day you'll convince your family to come to Dragons' Realm too.

Perhaps you'd like a longer adventure, starting a food fight, being caught by an archer, giving a dragonet chocolate or meeting tharuks – monsters roaming Dragons' Realm.

It is time to make a decision. Do you:

Go back to the park and escape the Thomson twins through the hole in the fence? **P3**

Go back to your last choice and let Bart Thomson die? **P187**

Go to the list of choices and start reading from another part of the story? **P206**

Or

Go back to the beginning and try another path? **P1**

More You Say Which Way Adventures.

Lost In Lion Country

Between the Stars

Danger on Dolphin Island

In the Magician's House

Secrets of Glass Mountain

Volcano of Fire

Once Upon an Island

The Sorcerer's Maze - Adventure Quiz

The Sorcerer's Maze - Jungle Trek

The Sorcerer's Maze - Time Machine

The Creepy House

YouSayWhichWay.com

List of Choices

More About the Author

Eileen Mueller lives in New Zealand, on the side of a hill, with her four dragonets.

In 2014 & 2015, she had lots of fun organizing Wellington's Storylines Family Day for thousands of kids – a festival bringing books alive through performances, crafts, and fun activities with kiwi authors and illustrators.

In her spare time, Eileen sings in a barbershop chorus, plants trees with school kids, and juggles her dragonets – usually without dropping them!

Dragons Realm is her first children's novel.

Eileen has many short stories published in anthologies. She is also:

- Sub-editor of *Lost in the Museum*, a young adult anthology which won the 2015 Sir Julius Vogel Award for Best Collected Work
- Co-editor of *The Best of Twisty Christmas Tales* a children's anthology, which includes stories by top NZ authors Joy Cowley and David Hill.
- Author of *Fairy Lights*, a short children's Christmas audio book.
- Shortlisted in the 2014 & 2015 Sir Julius Vogel Awards for writing, editing, and service.
- Winner of SpecFicNZ's Going Global award in 2013.
- Co-winner of NZ Society of Author's 2013 North-Write Collaboration literary award.

You can sign up for her reader's list,
or find more of her books at:
EileenMuellerAuthor.com

Made in the USA
Coppell, TX
27 February 2021

50971434R00125